ID0958264

Also by Enid Shomer

Tourist Season

Tourist Season

STORIES

ENID SHOMER

RANDOM HOUSE TRADE PAPERBACKS

NEW YORK

A Random House Trade Paperback Original

Copyright © 2007 by Enid Shomer
Reading group guide copyright © 2007 by Random House, Inc.

Published in the United States by Random House Trade Paperbacks, an imprint of The Random House Publishing Group, a division of Random House, Inc., New York.

RANDOM HOUSE TRADE PAPERBACKS and colophon are trademarks of Random House, Inc.
READER'S CIRCLE and colophon are trademarks of Random House, Inc.

The following stories have been previously published: "Fill In the Blank" in *Epoch,* "The Other Mother" in *Modern Maturity,* "The Summer of Questions" (under the title "Ask Me, Don't Ask Me") in *Paterson Literary Review,* "The Hottest Spot on Earth" in *Prairie Schooner,* "Rapture" in *Shenandoah,* "Tourist Season" in *Tikkun,* and "Chosen" in *Virginia Quarterly Review.*

ISBN 978-0-345-49442-9

Library of Congress Cataloging-in-Publication Data
Shomer, Enid.
Tourist season : stories / by Enid Shomer.
Random House trade pbk. ed.
p.   cm.
Contents: Chosen—The other mother—Fill in the blank—Tourist season—Rapture—The hottest spot on Earth—Sweethearts—Crash course—The summer of questions—Laws of nature.
ISBN 978-0-345-49442-9
1. Women—Fiction.   I. Title.
PS3569.H5783T68 2007
813'.54—dc22   2006045690

Printed in the United States of America

www.thereaderscircle.com

2 4 6 8 9 7 5 3 1

Book design by Victoria Wong

For Nirah H. Shomer and
Oren William Shomer

Contents

. . . what is it good for, I ask in all truth, a book that gives no recipes for mutton or for getting rid of fleas, . . . but which talks about a madman, by which I mean the world, that great idiot that has been rotating for so many centuries in space without moving forward a single step, and that howls and slobbers and tears itself apart.

—GUSTAVE FLAUBERT, *Memoirs of a Madman*

Better is one day in this life than a whole lifetime in the world to come.

—THE TALMUD

Tourist Season

Chosen

It was a Tuesday afternoon in early June. School had been out for a week. Iris's husband, Aaron, had settled a lamb roast in marinade, then taken the dog, Mimi, for a walk on the golf course. When the doorbell rang, Iris was reading *Harper's* and working a toothpick rhythmically in and out of her teeth. From her kitchen stool, she saw two dark shapes through the wavy glass panel of the front door.

She rose and peered through the peephole, her line of sight passing through the wooden door and then through the eye of the aluminum flamingo rampant on the screen door. Two bald heads tonsured with gray fringe swam into view, then two pale, placid faces and loosely knotted orange neckties framed by black lapels. "Yes?" she called through the closed door.

"Iris Hornstein," they said in unison. They were both slight, and looked vaguely Chinese. One was much shorter than the other.

"Yes."

The taller one opened the screen door, withdrew a business card from his pocket, and held it up to the peephole. Mr. Lu Something-or-other Sama. An address in Topeka. No, Tibet.

"What do you want?" Iris asked. She was suspicious of the matching black suits and limp, featureless white shirts. Mormon missionaries? Collectors for some charity she had never heard of? She pictured Tibetan orphans trudging up a snow-laced alpine path.

"To speak with you," Mr. Sama, the taller one, who seemed to be the spokesman, answered.

"I don't contribute to charities without reading about them first." Her rehearsed line, used for years with solicitors. "Do you have a brochure you could leave with me?" Her voice trailed off without conviction.

"We don't want money," the shorter one said, less patiently.

"Do we need an appointment?" Mr. Sama asked. "Oh, goodness," he fretted. "You are very busy at the present moment?"

The man was blushing, apparently at the thought that he had interrupted something important. They looked so sincere, and so unusual; she might as well see what they wanted. Aaron would be back in a few minutes, anyway. "No, I'm not very busy." She slid the deadbolt back, opened the door, and gestured toward the rattan sofa in the living room. "Come in."

"We bring you happy news." A smile creased the taller one's face, rounding his cheeks until they shined. Bowing slightly, the two men made their way through the doorway and sat side by side. Their smiles broadened into parades. Their eyes glimmered.

"How can I help you?" Iris asked, genuinely curious by now. Were they selling condo shares? Sweepstakes? Was there a Chinese lottery?

"We have an annunciation for you."

"You mean an *announcement*?" The correction was automatic. A speech therapist, Iris had spent her professional life listening to deflated vowels and blunted consonants, the pleadings of stutterers, not to mention simple mispronunciations.

The men turned to each other, silently conferring. "No. An *annunciation*," Mr. Sama insisted. Iris watched with some alarm as he unbuttoned his suit jacket and reached inside a narrow orange sash at his waist. It was the same brilliant shade as his tie, as the robes of those Buddhist monks who had immolated themselves—in Vietnam? Cambodia? Iris could not place the footage, but it played vividly in her mind, the protean orange of the monks' robes flying up in flames.

From the sash, Mr. Sama withdrew a colorful piece of cardboard, which unfolded downward, like a wallet pack of family photos. In a decorous tone, he began to read, glancing up periodically to make eye contact, as if he had learned public speaking from Dale Carnegie or the Toastmasters: "Based upon the words of the Dalai Lama, upon the sage writings of our Buddhist brothers and sisters, upon certain omens and signs given to us in dreams and in wakefulness, upon the mystical divination and divagation of soothsayers and mathematicians in Tibet, in India, and in Big Sur, California, and upon names and times written down with significance in his lifetime, it has been determined that Iris Hornstein is the reincarnation of the Great Adept, his holiness, the Saint Amarjampa." He took a breath. "You will assume your place, receive training in the ways of a Tibetan holy personage, and share your spiritual enlightenment." He jerked the paper accordion up, swatted it outward, and trapped it in his hand like a card sharp. The two men looked joyous. "You are this Iris Hornstein."

"I doubt it." She eyed the open door. Where was Aaron? "There must be more than one Iris Hornstein."

"Mother and father were Isador and Mildred Hornstein?"

"Yes."

"Born on February 13, 1948, in the city of Miami, in the state of Florida, in the U.S. of A.?"

"Yes." Iris suddenly remembered how the salesman had maneuvered her into buying her first car. She never had to say yes to the car itself, only to the features. She had bought power steering and sea green.

"At two fifty-three in the morning?"

"Two fifty-three? I really have no idea."

"It is written on your birth certificate," the short one said. "We have visited the courthouse."

"Oh," Iris said.

"*Om mani padme hum,*" Mr. Sama said.

"*Mani padme hum,*" Shorty echoed.

They rose and bowed, moving toward Iris like shy boys at a dance. Kneeling at her feet, they gently pried loose her hand clamped on the armrest of the chair and kissed it, closing their eyes reverently. When they opened them, they were full of tears.

―

Iris's only connection to Eastern religion was through her cousin Alta, who in the late sixties had lived for a year as a disciple in the ashram of Meher Baba, an Indian mystic famous, paradoxically, for his humility. Baba had taken a vow of silence for twenty years, spoke briefly from his sickbed, then died. A photo of this avatar had hung for years in her cousin's living room, looped with garlands of paper flowers and tin prayer wheels. Privately, Iris had mocked Baba, who reminded her of Danny Kaye with a goofy, mischievous gleam in his eye. In her cousin's glossy eight-by-ten, Baba was turning toward the camera energetically, his robes in a blur of motion, as if someone had just tapped him on the shoulder to deliver a telegram. His skin was taut and gleaming, his nose a thin white ridge with sculptural hollows on either side suggestive of privation. But he was grinning gleefully, as if about to burst into song and dance. A bony index finger pressed against his pursed lips, counseling silence in the interest of enlightenment or world peace or something that her cousin had never explained.

Iris didn't know why Alta had chosen an Indian ashram for her soul-searching instead of one of the communes that were popping up in the States. She decided the ashram was probably full of middle-aged American women. She imagined her cousin in a long gauzy skirt whisking along stone paths between huts while, in the center of the enclave, native women dished up braised offal afloat in lentil soup. Undoubtedly everyone wore sandals and bound their hair with wooden sticks and leather thongs. Although Alta regularly sent Iris postcards that barely withstood the mail and grew yeasty in the Florida heat, she had never really explained what she had been searching for or what she had found.

Not knowing what else to do, Iris offered the men iced tea. "Or would you rather have Coke?"

"We cannot allow you to serve us," Mr. Sama said, "Holiness."

"Look, I'm flattered, but there must be a mistake. I'm not even a Buddhist. And I'm certainly not Tibetan, as you can plainly see."

"You will learn whatever you need to know. Your soul is in a state of preparedness. You are full of wisdom."

Iris remembered the weird flashes at the health club she'd experienced lately while on the treadmill. Sometimes, during the endorphin rush, an assortment of hugely simplified statements or pert observations ticked across the screen of her mind, like headlines at Times Square. *Toothpicks prevent gum disease. . . . All concepts of honor are based on lack of birth control.* Or was it, *All concepts of honor are only a substitute for birth control. . . . Melons that smell ripe are rotten.* That sort of thing.

"You are a well of spiritual guidance."

"Then I hope you brought a bucket and a rope." Iris laughed at her own joke. The men blinked.

Was it possible? Iris didn't even believe in God, let alone reincarnation. "I don't believe in reincarnation," she blurted. At the same instant, the possibility that everything they had said might be true prodded at the edge of her mind, gently and hesitantly, like a kitten with its plump, soft paw.

Mr. Sama was not fazed. "It does not matter. Souls select their proper vessels. We shall teach you how to speak through the old soul and the new one together."

Shorty nodded his agreement.

"I have two souls?"

"We will come to all that." They smiled knowingly, affectionately, the way you might smile at a child who has mispronounced a word.

"I've heard the Dalai Lama is a wise, good man," Iris conceded. She'd seen the Dalai Lama on TV blessing a throng in Dharamsala, India. An American woman in the crowd had reported a surge of bliss when His Holiness touched her hand. "But I'm Jewish," Iris added.

"We know."

Shorty went to the kitchen and found three glasses and filled them with cold water. He opened the freezer and took out ice cubes. In the wire basket hanging above the sink where Iris kept vegetables and fruit, he found a single shrunken lemon and squeezed it into the water glasses. Iris realized with fright that she knew all this, though he was working behind her back, out of sight. Then she told herself it was natural for her to know it because she could hear him and there was nothing else but garlic and onions in the basket, so it was only logical to assume the lemon was—

"You left the door open," Aaron boomed, releasing Mimi from her leash and closing the front door. "I see we have company." He looked with bafflement at Iris in her chair and the small, dark-suited man kneeling at her feet. Mimi trotted over to Mr. Sama on the floor, licked his cheek once, and curled into her dog bed opposite the sofa.

Shorty said, "I will fix another glass of refreshment."

———

Ten years younger than Iris, Aaron was her third husband, and the only man she'd ever dated who was shorter than she was. (At five ten Iris had always felt unfeminine with shorter men.) He had a stocky body and curvy legs, like a Matisse figure, and lacked the competitive spirit and ambition that had destroyed her first two marriages. Back then, she couldn't have tolerated a man who worked less frantically than she. In the years when her life was divided between raising a young child, attending graduate school, and teaching part-time, Aaron had been a hippie dropout. He made macramé hammocks and plant holders (he had since moved on to stained glass) and smoked a lot of dope. He did not aspire to make a mark upon the world; in fact, he'd told Iris many times that he was trying to move through it without leaving a trace. They were both political idealists: Aaron threw his votes away on the Greens, while Iris was a yellow-dog Democrat. Aaron was naturally patient (some might say lazy), while Iris scribbled endless lists and did everything as if she were killing snakes. After twelve years of marriage, the two of them moved through their days like greased gears, coming together briefly for domestic chores and pleasures. They no longer remarked on each other's grating habits, though Iris's irritation with Aaron sometimes verged on rage. They had little left to fight about and little they were willing to fight about. This was the condition of their suffering and of their love.

Iris was not surprised that Aaron accepted the situation at face value, though he asked pointed questions: Why had it taken the monks so long to locate her? (It was the second time in three hundred years a saint had been reincarnated outside of Asia and in Iris's case all of the documents were in a foreign language—English.) Weren't most saints identified by the time they were eight or nine years old? (Yes. Iris was a special case. The saint's soul had been jittery and discontented, like a cobra kept in too small a basket.)

After the two men left, Aaron told Iris he was inclined to believe them because there were moments when she seemed otherworldly to him.

"Otherworldly?" Iris had echoed. "Do you mean I'm absent in some way?"

"No." He looked hurt at the suggestion that he was backhandedly criticizing her. "I mean, this is really weird, but when we make love, there's a kind of light that comes off your hair."

"Thank you, L'Oreal."

"I'm serious, Iris. Sometimes you look like you're glowing."

"It's probably just your astigmatism. You don't wear your glasses in bed."

"This is different. It's not a blur." He looked around the room for something to match the phenomenon he was trying to describe. "It's like the watery light you see above the highway—a mirage."

Aaron's stained-glass panels with their trapezoidal bands

of color and coronas projecting from the bodies of animals and plants owed much, Iris thought, to William Blake. She'd always thought these were metaphoric blasts of enlightenment, or symbolic representations of the souls of living things, but now she wondered if Aaron had a neurological disorder, something like migraine auras. He'd never complained of headaches, though. Was it possible that he actually saw these emanations of light? If he'd always seen them and thought it was normal, he might never have mentioned it. She remembered one of her clients, a seven-year-old boy who, after getting his first pair of glasses, asked what all the little green things on the trees were. Until that moment he'd seen the leaves as a solid blob.

"And it only happens when you're having an orgasm."

Iris looked for the telltale quiver in Aaron's nostrils that indicated he was putting her on, but his nose, like the rest of his face, was completely serious.

Lu and Wangrit, the Tibetan messengers, sat behind Iris in the charter jet, reading or quietly chatting. Incense burned in holders suction-cupped to windows on either side of the plane. At the rear, a shrine with statues of the Buddha and colorful wall hangings had been bolted to the floor. A billow of saffron silk on a circular shower curtain rod enclosed the devout. Or was it merely the meditative? Iris wondered. She slept and read; Aaron plotted designs on graph paper and worked his way through six back issues of *Art in America*. A young Tibetan in loose pants and a tunic offered food every three hours.

Though she didn't believe it factually, Iris operated on the premise that the dead—at least her dead—were sleeping in another dimension when she wasn't thinking about them. It was okay for them to sleep; she didn't feel obliged to animate them, like a ventriloquist. Whenever they appeared, it was like watching a Technicolor movie with extravagant period detail and surprising time-shifts. When the shape of her life was unclear or altering, instead of consulting a psychic, as some of her friends did, Iris imagined people from her past. And so it was that for the eighteen hours of Iris's flight to Tibet, Great Aunt Tanta, wearing Uncle's old black leather carpet slippers and a bargain-basement housedress, shuffled about preparing candied sweet potatoes for Rosh Hashana. The sweet potatoes clarified into a translucent orange sauce and then, like some miracle polymer, began to gleam and solidify. Tanta giggled at the chemistry as Iris and Alta lobbed it from hand to hand, then walked to opposite sides of the room to stretch it into long coppery ribbons. When cousin Alta had to make an emergency visit to the orthodontist two days later to repair her mangled braces, no one blamed Great Aunt Tanta, whom the adults considered an incorrigible old greenhorn, but who, Iris and Alta knew, was only playing dumb for their benefit.

Iris studied the sky through her window of the plane. Something was different as they flew west from San Francisco into tomorrow. The sun took forever to set, its coral and pink banners awash in the clouds for nearly an hour. At last the sky turned ink blue; a few stars pierced it, then all was black.

"When we see the sun, we will almost be home," Lu, the taller one, said. Iris had not noticed him standing nearby.

"What if you've made a mistake?" she asked.

"You do not have to think you are wise to be wise."

"But what if I am really stupid?" Iris pressed.

"Perhaps no one has asked you the right questions."

She thought for a second. "But then you, the questioners, are the wise ones," she countered, "aren't you?"

Lu touched her shoulder. He glanced at Wangrit, who was watching the interchange. The two men smiled at each other, then at Iris. It was a benevolent and soothing smile, in no way smug. Perhaps Iris did possess wisdom she was not aware of, perhaps it was waiting to be tapped, like a vein of precious ore, by the right sharp inquiry. Maybe age had something to do with it, conferring a sheen easily mistaken for mere wear, like the objects on *Antiques Roadshow* that seemed to change right before your eyes once they were set upon a baize-covered table and identified as antiques.

Now Tanta straightened the antimacassars on the seat backs in the plane, her breasts moving in their own rhythm a few beats behind, like a sign language interpreter. They were enormous breasts, mute and impressive as mountains. Iris wished she could write an ode to old breasts, but instead patted her own: though lower on her body than ever, they were still small, as if they had not yet fulfilled their destiny, unlike Tanta's, which had developed into something very different—sagacious, more planetary. Tanta—she would have made a credible Tibetan saint. Who but a saint could have wielded a pointer for thirty years at the Orthodox Jewish school while class after class of fifteen-year-olds gawked at her breasts swinging in the opposite direction? What but holiness could account for Tanta as she lighted the Sabbath candles, her breasts echoing the circling motion of her hands over the flames?

Tibet was a place of crisp air, bells, and snails. The mollusks threaded through every patch of green and brown, tacking like tiny ships on slender silver currents. Above them, nothing fashioned by human hands challenged the soaring landscape. Herds of goats, sheep, and yaks grazed on the dewy grasses, moving as slowly as shadows as they wandered across the river valley and into the village.

Aaron's only hesitation about going to Tibet was that he didn't want to miss the baseball season, which, Iris knew, supplied texture and rhythm to his life for six months of every year. The Tibetans bought him a shortwave radio so that he could hear his White Sox and Yankee games in real time. Iris, employed by the school system, was off for the summer, and had requested a leave for the fall term. Everyone but her daughter believed Iris and Aaron had found a fabulous cut-rate vacation package to Thailand.

In a village far from Lhasa, Iris and Aaron were installed in a lodge once used for traveling foreign Buddhists. It was spacious and comfortably appointed, with pale yellow gauze curtains, bright area rugs, and two indoor waterfalls. Massive half timbers supported expansive glass walls. Next door, at the monastery, a small brotherhood cooked, prayed, and tended the grounds.

It was a lonely life. Iris's identity was to be kept secret for three or four months until she was transferred to the community in exile in Dharamsala, India. A half dozen young boys, recent refugees in Buddha, their newly shaved heads still pale, waved at her every afternoon from the courtyard, but otherwise the only people she and Aaron saw were Lu and Wangrit and the monks who served them. Lu promised that Iris would soon have more company than she knew what to do with. "You will greet the multitude," he said.

Iris tried to picture this event: seated on a low gilt throne bracketed on either side with temple urns, she would be the epicenter from which orange and yellow carpet runners streamed in all directions, like sunbeams. She'd wear a brocade caftan and feathered turban. In her hand, variously, a scepter, a gong, a walking stick, a walkie-talkie. No. She would dress in her native costume: a three-season suit from Eileen Fisher and black leather boots.

She had expected to be deluged upon arrival with tracts on philosophy and religion, but not a single idea per se had been presented to her. Instead of catechism, she'd been given book after illustrated book from the large, eclectic collection of the Dalai Lama. There was no apparent method to the selections. Lu and Wangrit arrived every couple of days lugging boxes from the library. Just study the pictures, Lu had told her. In the first week, she paged through European medieval strap work, scent and snuff bottles, Roman coins, the fossil history of the horse and elephant, Neolithic burial sites, and the carved ivories and jades of the Far East. The second week brought antique sewing implements, orchids of West Africa, the ancient city of Cappodocia, the lives of bees, Renaissance costumes, a botanical survey of Antarctica, and *Rotifers: The World in a Drop of Water.*

She consumed this material while on a treadmill. Why not? Iris had thought, when Lu asked her if she desired anything special from home. Walking oxygenated the brain. Or as Lu had said, it "purified the breath." As far as Iris could tell, the Tibetans regarded the breath with the same fearful reverence her mother had once reserved for the bowel movement: both were considered essential, had to be expelled regularly, and reflected the condition of the whole body—possibly even of the soul.

Each morning while temple bells rolled golden hoops of sound into the clear Tibetan air, Iris walked, never departing or arriving, leaving no tracks. Sometimes, to wipe the slate clean, she looked up from her books to gaze at the mountains resolving into shades of purple in the distance. At the end of each session, her mind, like a stomach after a huge repast, was uncomfortably full, roiling with distorted images of what it had devoured: lace made of Pacific krill; skyscrapers instead of stamens and pistils rising from the mouths of flowers. And, day after day, like an inefficient generator that is fed on the raw power of a lightning storm and gives back only minuscule sparks of electricity, her brain produced peripatetic fizzles of thought. *The inventor of nonslip tile should receive the Nobel Prize. . . . The cause of the Second World War was the First World War. . . . Cookbooks make you hungry. . . . In Scandinavia, do brunettes have more fun?*

In the second month, Lu switched her from sight to sound. She heard soloists and choruses, orchestras and ensembles, the songs of whales and the crackling of insect traffic on the jungle floor, howler monkeys howling, and the mechanical dither of mating dragonflies. Though Aaron sampled the books and tapes, he had nowhere near Iris's capacity for absorption. She was becoming a sponge, a satellite dish, a receiver for all that could be seen and heard in the world. Great Aunt Tanta, shaped by the discipline of teaching school and the piety of keeping kosher had, in life, always been on the move. Now, though, when Iris thought her back into existence, Tanta was alone and unoccupied. She hovered near the treadmill or sat in a chair, her hands folded in her lap, her face expressionless, as if she were daydreaming Iris into the world.

At the end of the second month, while Iris was listening to masted ships in the wind and the Turkish Mehter, the world's first marching band, Aaron took a three-day guided trek out of the valley, onto the plateau. There, at fourteen thousand feet, amid the arid, howling winds, he discovered the tents of the nomads hunkered down, patient and black as crows, their pointed tops sticking up like ruffled feathers. Wind- and waterproof, the tents were woven of yak hair on the outside, while colorful embroidered plants and animals danced across the felt lining inside. These tents, Aaron told Iris excitedly, were going to be the first black objects he ever incorporated in a piece of stained glass. "I'm calling it *Tent Mandala,*" he said.

"But no light will come through."

"Almost none. That's how it is—no light, no sound. You've got to see it, Iris. Inside, it's like a padded room."

Iris sighed, the sound of a saw blade complaining in the wood. "I've been reading the *Tibetan Book of the Dead*."

"Finally," Aaron said. "Great!"

"Great? Have you read it?"

"I'm not quite sure," Aaron said. That was what he always said when he wanted to avoid bluntly saying no. Sometimes it drove Iris wild. She waited while he checked his memory banks. She knew that in his hippie days he'd followed a girlfriend through a brief flurry of Buddhism and taken a comparative religion course at Florida State. He'd already told her he hadn't learned much beyond the superficial: Buddhist countries had more temples than telephone booths; big raft, little raft—nothing Iris hadn't encountered in her speed-reading at the Leesburg Public Library the week before they left for Tibet. "No," he finally said. "I don't think so."

"It's instructions for dying. If your last thoughts aren't right, your soul gets sent back to the wrong body."

"Gee," Aaron said. "I didn't know the Buddhists were so uptight."

On an afternoon so overcast the daylight was made of pure glare, the foursome sat in the lodge drinking butter tea, the national concoction, out of tin cups. Iris had been in Tibet for nearly three months and she felt no wiser than when she arrived. "When do I learn to be my saint?" she asked Lu and Wangrit.

"The Buddha became enlightened while sitting under a fig tree, doing nothing," Wangrit told her evenly.

"You are learning already," Lu said. "You are learning the world so that you can leave it with ease."

"The world of elephant tusks and algae?" Iris heard the sarcasm edging her voice, but she didn't care.

"Patience was never Iris's strong suit," Aaron told the two men.

Aaron was right. She was energetic, not patient. But if they were simply testing her patience, why all the books and tapes? She flopped down in an armchair. She was sick of second-guessing everyone's motives. "What's this doing here, anyway?" she demanded.

"What?" Lu asked, alarmed.

"This stupid chair. What's a stupid Cape Cod armchair doing in Tibet?" She felt her throat tightening. "What am I doing in Tibet?" Now, damn it, she was going to cry.

"Oh, babe." Aaron put his arms around her.

"I still know absolutely nothing about my old soul. Or my new one. Or Buddhism, for that matter."

Aaron stroked her neck.

"None of you are any help to me." Iris sniffed.

Lu and Wangrit, eyes glistening, cocked their heads ever so slightly. Like concerned cocker spaniels, Iris thought.

"Poor baby," Aaron said. He appeared distraught, as if he might start blubbering, too. Sometimes Aaron's emotions surfaced too easily to count for much in Iris's eyes. And in her blackest moods, she thought him something of a fool—too kindhearted, liable to let people take advantage of him. What other forty-nine-year-old man schlepped his friends to the airport and back? But this tenderness was also what she loved in him. She stifled the urge to tell him to shove his empathy.

"Oh! There's a Buddhist pitch in baseball." Aaron brightened. "I forgot about that. The knuckleball."

Lu and Wangrit inched forward in their chairs.

"Not even the pitcher knows exactly where it's going. It depends on the wind. It's all about release and loss of control."

Iris imagined planet Earth slowly wobbling out of orbit, like a bowling ball headed for the gutter. "But none of the players are Buddhists, are they?"

"I wish Darryl Strawberry had become a Buddhist instead of a Christian," Aaron opined. "No, it's the commentators. They like to elevate the game by throwing around philosophical terms. They talk about the Zen of baseball, too."

Lu put his hands together in a prayerful pose. "Desire is the cause of suffering, and enlightenment is the cure. That is all you need to know for now."

"Or forever," Wangrit added.

"That's right," Aaron recalled. "Buddha said suffering didn't come from the outside world or an evil figure like Satan, but from the individual mind."

Iris perked up a little. "That's good. So you could say he was the world's first psychiatrist."

"There you go, babe." Aaron smiled tentatively at her.

"I better not find out he had a hundred wives while he was getting rid of his desire. But tell me"—she turned to Lu and Wangrit—"Why did the monks make a butter sculpture of the Buddha's head yesterday?" She told them she'd seen one leaving the kitchen of the monastery. "It was elaborate, with long curls and an embroidered hat."

"A real hat?" Aaron asked.

"No, a butter hat."

"Weird," Aaron said.

"Yeah," Iris said. "It looked pretty wasteful to me. Wasteful and luxurious. And you can't have luxury without desire." The butter sculpture had upset her. She didn't want to believe it was the Tibetan equivalent of an American televangelist's gold-plated bathroom sink. "What I'm wondering"—Iris stared at Lu, then Wangrit—"is whether the monks are going to eat it," she hesitated, her voice cold as ice, "or rub their feet with it." Tanta stood on the treadmill, not moving, her good ear pointed toward the group. Lu and Wangrit regarded Iris calmly.

"I want to show you something," Lu said.

Everyone was sitting around the tea tray. Lu lifted the lid on a squat ceramic jar. "Look how much yak butter we have here."

"Butter everywhere in Tibet," Wangrit said.

"Butter is cheap." Lu stirred a large dollop into the teapot. Iris watched it liquefy into small golden globules. "We eat it the way the Chinese eat rice."

"So much butter we burn it in our lamps, rub it on our skin," Wangrit told her. "Women braid their hair with it."

Iris felt ashamed. "I'm sorry."

Lu said, "You do not have to apologize when you ask questions."

Iris gave each of them a brief hug. It was the first time she had touched them. Their bodies were thin and cool through their saffron robes.

After returning from India, cousin Alta had moved on to other things, primarily appliances. Her house sparkled with gadgets to make life easier: blender; mixer; curling iron; bread machine; pasta, yogurt, and rice makers; floor waxer; convection oven. "I have a right to be happy," Alta had said. "That's what I learned in India. I have a right." Iris thought that if Alta used all these labor- and time-saving devices, she'd end up busy and miserable every minute of the day. But Alta didn't use them. Instead, she admired them in their pristine state, like a stamp collection. Then, in 1980, something (Iris never learned what) had cast a shadow on the sweeping vistas of stainless steel and Formica. Alta, never particularly political, packed her belongings into two suitcases and joined the campaign of the independent presidential candidate John Anderson. She worked on Anderson's advance team, lining up hotel rooms and restaurants, buying balloons by the gross. She died in a car accident on her way to rent a sound system for a rally in Ft. Collins, Colorado.

Iris's moment with the multitude was at hand.

After nearly four months in Tibet, she, Aaron, Lu, and Wangrit flew to Dharamsala, then rested for a day. Lu calmed her. Expect nothing, he said. All she had to do was meet a couple of hundred people—including monks, Buddhist priests or lamas, a few nuns, and some lesser rinpoches—and accept the presentation scarves they would deposit ceremoniously at her feet.

Lu and Wangrit escorted her and Aaron into a large, tiled shrine room in the temple where the multitude had assembled. As she crossed the room, the crowd divided as neatly as the Red Sea to form a path for her, then closed behind her as quickly as it had parted. "Am I glowing now?" she whispered to Aaron, wide-eyed and joyous by her side.

It was customary for incarnated lamas to be higher than everyone else in the room, so a chair elevated on a dais had been arranged. But Iris towered over everyone and simply stood most of the time. They addressed her as Holiness. They didn't test her or try to extract information. A palpable warmth suffused the room—something like love—and it lifted her like a bird on a thermal updraft. I am honored to be among you, she repeated, bowing a little when they bowed. Lu translated for her, going on at length though she said only this. Tanta watched from a corner, puffed up with pride.

Then the four of them were whisked into a small chamber inside the gilt summit of the temple. Below, on the ground, pilgrims circled the building counterclockwise as they chanted *om mani padme hum*—Hail the jewel in the lotus flower! Suddenly the Dalai Lama was standing beside her, surrounded by men and women of all races. They enclosed him, moving precisely together, like a team of performers inside an elephant costume. Chairs appeared and everyone sat. Tea was served, and small bittersweet cookies. The Dalai Lama spoke English, but occasionally addressed his cohorts in other languages.

He and Iris exchanged pleasantries about the weather in Florida, Tibet, and Sweden, where the Dalai Lama had just spent several weeks. He was forced to travel a great deal, especially since receiving the Nobel Prize. "They say you live in an airplane," Iris said. "Is that true?"

He smiled. "I live in Tibet."

She looked at him with disbelief. Everyone knew that he had been in exile since the Chinese occupation of Tibet in 1950.

"There is a curiosity of language here," he explained. "Do you know what the Tibetan word for Tibet is?"

"I'm sorry," Iris said. "I really don't."

"It's 'Bet.' So then you see that your English word 'Tibet' sounds to me as if it means to Tibet, or toward Tibet. On the way to Tibet."

Something innately marvelous and sad was about to be revealed, Iris felt.

"So I could answer quite accurately, using your language, that I live in Tibet, whether I am on an airplane, or here in India, or in Sweden. I am always going toward Tibet, in one way or another. In my heart, certainly."

Iris pondered the significance of *Tibet*.

"We wish you also to live in the place of your heart, Iris."

"Florida," she said, without hesitating. "Oh, I like Tibet and India immensely—"

"That is our wish for you, too. You will be a bridge between the two cultures. Lu will interrogate and translate. He will be your bright eye. Wangrit will assist you both." It was a question, not a statement. His face lay open, waiting for her reply. She agreed.

From the box of puppets in Iris's office, Riley, age eight, chose a red plush dog with a happy felt mouth that opened and closed. Iris often used hand puppets in her sessions to distract a child's stuttering brain and give his voice a way out.

She placed a globe of the world in front of the boy. "Can the puppy say hello to England?" She pointed to a pink splotch. Riley touched it with the puppet. "Hell!" he yelled, "O England!" Riley moved the puppet across the world, nipping at the continents and seas. Tanta sat behind him in the sunlit alcove of the bay window playing solitaire. Through the window, Iris noticed that Aaron had left his studio door open. His huge *Tent Mandala* stained glass resembled a flock of crows scattering into the sky.

Iris had devised a game for Riley, using words and pictures of foreign lands she had fashioned into flash cards. She began reciting the list Riley liked best because he thought the words sounded funny. *Yak*, she said. He repeated the word and collected the picture from the stack. *Yurt*, she continued. *Snow, goat, tea. Buddhist, Temple, Tibet.*

Riley stuttered twice, both times severely—long noisy chains of hard "G's" dragged through *gong* and a salvo of "T's" in *temple*.

"Riley, do you want to walk Mimi before you go?" Iris asked. Ever since returning from Iris's daughter's house, where she had played nonstop with the grandkids, Mimi had been starved for attention from children. Riley raced to the back porch, hooked Mimi to her leash, and banged through the door. Iris could hear him singing on the side walkway. That was one of the mysteries of stuttering: it disappeared completely in songs and in sleep. No one stammered in dreams.

She shifted her focus to the patio. Lu and Wangrit were lounging by the pool, listening to a game on the radio. They had become Yankee fans. She had finally convinced them to wear American-style bathing trunks, though they had insisted on identical ones. Now Lu tipped his navy baseball cap to her. Tonight, after dinner, she would review her day, guided by his questions—not as a summary, but in the way you might muse about a half-remembered dream, spinning out fantasies and significances. Lu would record everything in his lotus-paper notebook. In the predawn, she might wake to find them chanting poolside, or munching on celery stalks with butter.

Iris gazed at the Florida sky, which was pale compared to the intense, deep blue of Tibet. She knew the difference had to do with the high altitude. Tibetan air was so thin that early explorers claimed to have seen the stars at noon from the highest peaks. But these accounts, like the reports of temples made of solid gold and sightings of Yeti, the Himalayan Bigfoot, turned out to be travelers' tales.

The Other Mother

Sheila works for $5.50 an hour at Dillard's Department Store, in her first paying job. For two weeks now she has sold Finer Apparel. Finer than what? Not finer than the dresses she left in Mobile. Not finer than her grandmother's wedding gown, enlarged with gores of satin and lace so that she could wear it when she married Selwyn. Not fine enough for her daughter, Royal, sixteen, who sports a ring on every finger, like her mother. It's killing Sheila that Royal didn't run away from Mobile with her. "My heart is in splinters," she told the crisis hotline from a pay phone on University Avenue in Gainesville, a college town red-roofed with Pizza Huts and motels. "I had to leave my daughter behind," Sheila told the crisis counselor. "She didn't want to come with me just yet. She's adopted." At least Royal isn't living with Selwyn.

Sheila works in vertical merchandising, meaning that each day she freshens the racks pawed over by customers and touches up wrinkled blouses with a steamer. All the blouses are white, identical except for price and small details indistinguishable from a distance: shawl collar, tuxedo pleats, princess seaming. Eventually the French cuffs will fray. Eventually the blouses will age into rags.

Sheila herself is like a piece of fine fabric that has been shredded. For three weeks she's been on the run. That's how she thinks of it, though she has come to a dead stop on the floor of her nephew's apartment where she sleeps on an air mattress, covered only with a sheet.

Three is her lucky number. When she left Mobile she grabbed three skirts, three pairs of slacks, three framed photographs of Royal. The counselor on the hotline had asked her if she was thinking of killing herself. "Not until you mentioned it just now," Sheila said, perfectly serious. The counselor gave her another phone number, urged her to call anytime. "Use a pseudonym," the counselor added. "Gainesville isn't that big a town."

If Sheila were Catholic, she would confess her sin every day, willingly accept a harsh penance, hope for a portion of forgiveness. But she is Presbyterian, spiked with brimstone Baptist. There is a hell, and she and Selwyn are going there.

Sheila had watched birth videos before they adopted Royal. All those grimacing little boys and girls, their newborn faces pressed flat. Babies looked so much alike except for hair and skin color. A few days later their faces plumped back up. Royal must have looked like that after she was squeezed out with fear and pain from the other mother's body, before she was handed to Sheila, who had been waiting to adopt for years.

As Sheila moves through her day in Finer Apparel, she keeps mental track of Royal's routine. Now Royal is slamming her locker shut at school in the clamor before classes start. Now her hands are fluttering above her food as she talks to a boy in the cafeteria. Royal didn't leave town with her mother because she didn't want to change schools. She is living with Sheila's mother in a seniors' condo where potted palms froth up in the lobby beneath huge ceiling fans. Sheila's mother is a thin, stylish woman held together with hair spray, Chanel No. Five, and Rebel Yell bourbon. She has trouble ordering from menus and doesn't watch the evening news or read the paper. Sheila never could confide in her mother without worrying about wounding her. Sheila's mother is selfish, not from arrogance, but from weakness. She is too frail to shoulder anyone else's problems, even someone she loves.

Sheila is a better parent, that's clear, though she now realizes she's sometimes been a touch careless, turning her back on Royal in her carriage, letting go of her pudgy hand in shopping malls and restaurants. She tries to recall every instance of imperfect vigilance: in the homes of friends, on her back porch, in the yard. And even at the airport, just like the other mother. Sheila imagines the other mother constantly now: sitting at a table with her back to Sheila, her shoulders are rounded, her body sagging in a series of interrupted curves. Sheila moves closer, but she cannot picture the woman's face. The face has been eroded, washed away by anguish.

—

The day before Sheila ran away, Win came home from work at one o'clock in the afternoon, headed straight to the bedroom, and began drinking bourbon. When Sheila walked in, he was lying on the bed, staring at the ceiling. The radio was on and people were phoning in their opinions of former President Nixon, who had just died. He weakened the presidency. He invented "dirty tricks" and changed the course of politics forever, Sioux City said.

"What's wrong?" Sheila asked.

"Everything," Win said.

Nixon was a lesson in perseverance. He paid for his mistakes. (How? Sheila wondered. Why didn't he go to jail?) He outlived his own shame until it aged into something finer, something called courage, said Austin, Texas.

"But what specifically is wrong?" How was today different from yesterday? Sheila wondered.

"I'm going to leave you," Win said. He looked remorseful.

"Oh God, Win. You can't. It'll break Royal's heart." That really was the first thing Sheila thought. Sheila would be okay. She'd join a singles group, get a job—any kind of job—place an ad in the Heart-to-Heart classifieds: *DWF ISO sincere WM, 40–50, for real commitment.*

"Don't bring Royal into it. She'll get over it. A lot of kids' parents get divorced."

"But not twice."

The call-in show was heating up: Nixon was either a criminal or a saint. Win switched off the radio. "We're not married, remember?"

Selwyn was slick. Selwyn was smooth, his body glossy as the inside of a shell, each muscle sleek, the skin slipping over it. In high school, his friends nicknamed him "Win" and it stuck. His signature made a dashing, cavalier impression on the page, like a stylishly tipped hat. *Love and kisses, Win. Thinking of you, Win,* as if cheering her to some victory.

They had met in Mobile, at a reunion for the Trewsdale Academy, a stronghold of castlelike buildings and wide lawns shaded by live oaks. They were both Trewsdale graduates, but hadn't known each other during their school days. Six months later they married.

Win depleted his inheritance in a succession of showy, volatile businesses. Broker of yachts and berthage. Importer of parrots from Surinam and alabaster from Turkey. When his fortune eroded to three-quarters of a million, he bought into a silver- and copper-mining company. He worked out of one of Mobile's courtly Painted Ladies converted to offices. Headquarters was in a scrappy old building farther downtown, near the port. In return for his investment, he was put in charge of Asian operations. He flew to India, where the mines were small and primitive. He suspected the translators of intentionally making him look like a fool.

Win kept Sheila on a cash allowance for the house and food. For everything else, she had two gold cards, both canceled now. The day after she left Win, she was as poor as a sparrow. It made her feel noble and desperate at the same time. Money could do that—sweep you up and drop you like a tornado. Most of Sheila's life it was a given. Now she senses its lack at every turn in surprising, humiliating ways that make her feel spoiled and unworthy. Her hair, for example, was highlighted just before she left Mobile. Now she'll have to use drugstore color. Her head will be all one shade, like a wall.

Sheila misses the exquisite moments of pleasure that money bought. Her beaded minidress like granulated gold, the antique lorgnette for a necklace. They were going to a gala benefit for the Children's Society. Downstairs, Win waited in his classic jet tuxedo, a silhouette of corners tapering to points. Two rooms away, in her crib, Royal slept her moist, perfumed sleep. Sheila primped at her vanity, the smoke from her cigarette climbing the air in slow spirals. A glass of good Scotch sat beside the cosmetic tray, a skyline of lipstick tubes and assorted wands. She took a last glimpse in the mirror as she pushed the chair back along the dense wool carpet and caught herself, nearly unaware, nearly someone else.

The car was clean and waxed. She slid into her leather seat. It wasn't true that things couldn't make you happy. Things had made her happy for fifteen years. When she clothes-shopped in September and March, the salesgirls brought in sandwiches and lemonade on folding tables, always with nice touches—straw flowers in a vase, a fanciful glass stirrer. She never thought of them as bootlickers. Their behavior was natural. You should be nice to someone who is going to spend a lot of money.

Most days after work, Sheila retreated to Watermelon Lake before returning to her nephew's. Located on the campus of the agricultural college, it was fringed with live oaks and caught the sunsets in its golden clasp. It was beautiful and safe; the university police patrolled it twenty-four hours a day. No one had ever disappeared from its shores despite alligators thrashing the water and vagabonds spilling out like human refuse on the lawns. She could think there, think in short bits, like breathing. She could hold her breath over the worst parts.

She and Win had tried for six years to have a baby, practiced positioned, passionless sex according to a calendar. Win blushed, left alone in a doctor's cubicle with *Playboy, Hustler,* and a plastic cup. His sparse sperm wagged across a glass slide. He took vitamins and worked out. He took vitamins and rested. He switched from jockeys to boxer shorts as the doctor advised.

They went to Houston for in vitro fertilization. Several slow tadpoles pierced eggs that had been surgically removed from Sheila, but the eggs did not divide. They sat like small dented basketballs under the bright gaze of the microscope. The doctor tried to be comforting. It was probably a blessing in disguise, he claimed, a sign of genetic incompatibility. If an egg had developed, it might have been terribly deformed.

They signed up to adopt a baby, but the waiting list was long. They wanted a white baby, a baby that looked like them. Win believed that Mobile wasn't ready for a mixed baby.

Nevertheless, he agreed to look at a light-skinned biracial infant. When Sheila stared into the child's unflinching brown eyes, her insides tightened, as if she had stage fright. The baby's hair curled like gift ribbon from his perfect skull. "He's beautiful," Win admitted, "but his hair's too frizzy. He'll always be hassled." He handed the infant back to his caretaker. "I can't change the world."

Sheila was quiet.

"We're going to get a baby," Win insisted. "I promise you, we're going to have our own baby."

The list of infertile couples grew longer, babies scarcer. Someone at a houseboat party passed them a card with the name of a clinic in Mexico, but of course a Mexican baby would stand out, too. They threw away the card.

One day, Win came home from work ebulliently bearing a sheaf of delphiniums and irises, the stems so long he held the bouquet away from his body, like a torch. He'd heard of a doctor in Georgia who managed a lot of private adoptions.

It probably wasn't entirely legal, but Sheila didn't care about that anymore. She stood in the kitchen, snipping the stems, inserting them into a globe of floral foam in tall clusters like rays. If some girl in Georgia was desperate enough to give up or sell her baby, Sheila was going to take it.

Royal was perfect. She looked like Sheila, her eyes the same hazel wheels with flecks of gold in them. Win insisted on going to get the baby by himself. Sheila didn't question him. *Mommy,* Sheila thought. *Mommy and Daddy.* After Win brought Royal home, Sheila drove downtown to Posh Baby and paid for the opulent layette she had reserved the week before in both pink and blue. When Royal was old enough to understand, they would tell her she was adopted. All the official records would be sealed under the weight of time, like a pharaoh in his tomb.

They never talked about the adoption again. Win gave me a baby, Sheila thought. That is how she always thought of Royal—as a love child.

—

If Sheila ever met Royal's natural mother, what could she say to her? *Possession. Possession is nine-tenths of the law.* Sheila would do anything for this unknown woman, anything except give up Royal. *I'm so sorry,* she rehearses. *Ashamed. Kill me. Go ahead and kill me, I'd understand. But of course it would be terrible for Royal. I'm the only mother she knows.*

—

Win began smoking and drinking heavily. He had always been a social drinker, but now he got smashed several days a week. Some nights he didn't come home.

A silent rage inundated Sheila, expressing itself in more perfect meals, more expertly applied makeup, evenings out with women friends several times a month to give the illusion of greater independence. She expected Win to leave her, but he didn't. She decided to wait it out rather than confront him. She believed he'd come around.

He stopped sleeping with her. Sheila considered having an affair, but no one suitable came to mind. She and Win focused on Royal and on extravagant distractions. At Christmas, they bought real gold tinsel for the tree. At Easter, the three of them vacationed in Austria. Dinners at home became elaborate. Sheila knew that expensive food brought out their best manners and camouflaged charged silences at the table as mere formality.

On their twenty-first wedding anniversary, just a month before Win left, Sheila served a catered meal followed by imported cheeses and a rare brandy. Royal had brought a date. After dinner, she and the boy were in the den choosing CDs to listen to.

"I don't like the look of him," Win said. They had been arguing about the boy ever since he arrived. "It isn't a matter of trusting Royal, it's a matter of trusting a stranger with more than hands in his pockets."

Sheila set down her snifter. "I trust Royal's *judgment*. She knows this boy from school."

"You knew me from school," Win pointed out sarcastically.

"And now you don't like the look of me, either!" She spit out the words like bitter medicine. "Win, I never thought you'd stop loving me."

"I still love you," Win protested. "I do."

She looked at him with surprise, her face burning. "Then why don't you want to make love to me?"

"I'm sorry," Win said. "I can't talk about this. I'll never be able to talk about it."

━━

The divorce went smoothly. The only thing Win insisted on was joint custody, which Sheila agreed to. Win adored Royal.

He'd protect her with his money and his life. She wanted Royal to have that affection and security.

Four months after the final decree, Win approached Sheila about borrowing money on the house. Once they began to talk about finances, about survival, a comfortable familiarity returned. They mortgaged the house to the hilt to save one of the teetering mines in India, and celebrated the risk by making love all night. Toward dawn, Sheila lay facedown on the bed and Win lay on top of her, in a position he always called "the stationary massage." His naked body pressed against hers; she sank into the deep contours of the feather bed. Her chest heaved against his weight, as if she'd traveled to a planet where the atmosphere had the density of flesh. He'd never meant to stop wanting her. If it happened again, he'd see a counselor or sex therapist. His tears dripped down her shoulders. The effort to breathe against the weight of his body and his grief was satisfying though bittersweet, as if she had won an argument she had hoped would prove her wrong.

He moved back in. Royal was elated. They celebrated their reunion with a vacation in Bermuda. It was terribly expensive and Sheila worried about Win spending so freely. It seemed that money was the only way he could show his love that wasn't accompanied by pain. A gift required no reasons, no apologies, no plans for the future.

The reunion faltered, deteriorating after several months into the pattern that had led to the divorce—Win drinking heavily again, staying out at night. This time, Royal took it all in. And though she said nothing to her mother, Sheila sensed Royal's sadness and fear at the breakfast and dinner table as

Royal's gaze shifted from her mother's passive face to her father's empty chair.

———

The day before Sheila bolted from Mobile, when Win told her he was leaving her for the second time, he also finally told her the truth about Royal.

They were in the bedroom, the place where they now argued instead of making love. In the background, the phone-in program about Nixon was heating up. Sheila pointed out that few parents divorced twice. He had switched off the radio and reminded her that they weren't married.

Of course, Sheila thought. It only *felt* like they were married. Still, something must have changed, something invisible and terrible had twisted Win's heart again. "Win, I love you," she begged. "Whatever it is, we can work it out. We can."

"No. We *can't*," Win corrected her.

The next part of the conversation, a barrage of nasty, cutting remarks from Win, was too awful to remember precisely. He had nothing but contempt for her, he couldn't stand the sight of her, and more. The next clear words came from Sheila. They were "our Royal."

"Our Royal?" Win laughed bitterly. "You know Royal isn't really ours." He lit another cigarette.

"Well, of course I know that. She's adopted."

"You're so dumb. I think you choose to be dumb."

"What are you talking about?"

"Royal's not adopted," Win said. He watched Sheila's face.

"I'm not so dumb," Sheila said. "It occurred to me that somehow you might have . . ." She paused to find the least painful word. "Somehow you might have *negotiated* for her."

"You mean bought her?"

"I don't know, Win. I don't know what you did."

"I didn't buy her." Win inhaled deeply from his cigarette and held his breath until his face reddened.

"Oh, thank God. I figured you found some sleazy doctor who told a poor girl it was legal to pay more than her medical—"

"I stole her."

The muscles in Sheila's body tightened all at once, as if someone had pulled a drawstring.

"That's right. She was kidnapped." Win was completely drunk and talking fast now. Tears coursed down his cheeks. "I didn't personally do it. I hired a couple of guys. I told them what kind of baby to look for and left the rest up to them. They took her from a restroom at the Memphis airport. One of them dressed in drag to do it."

Sheila collapsed into the wing chair in the corner of the bedroom.

"The mother went into a toilet stall and left Royal parked outside in a stroller a few feet away, in front of the sinks. No, not the sinks." Win struggled to paint the scene. "In front of a counter where women were combing their hair. It happened fast."

At seven-thirty it is still light out. Sheila drives to Watermelon Lake, unfolds herself from the car, and crunches down the gravel path to a picnic bench. The wind is blowing the azalea petals off the bushes. In a few weeks, she'll have enough money to rent a place. Her mother and Royal will visit, her mother's head held stiff and high above the rising water of Sheila's life, Royal appalled by Sheila's mingy quarters. Sheila will flap loudly between them for two or three days, like a broken screen door.

"If you loved me, really loved *me,* you'd have been suspicious instead of selfish," Win had screamed. "You'd have shared the guilt." He'd spared Sheila the truth all those years, and now he hated her for it.

Win was a criminal. Maybe he kept it secret because he thought she wouldn't have gone along with it. Maybe he thought she might use it against him someday. Sheila's mind can't track all the possibilities. She wants Royal beside her now. Royal, please God, biting the polish off her nails, lobbying for a cashmere sweater from J. Crew, threatening to go to New York City instead of to college.

The sun drops into the lake, the water fades from molten red to rust. There's only the sound of dark waves probing the shore. She'll go back to Mobile, it's just a matter of time. A year, maybe less. To protect Royal, the rest of Sheila's life must be a lie, a lie that fills her chest like a heavy, dead second heart. She can never tell anyone. The lie is a kind of eternity that will outlive everyone who suffered or profited from it. She must teach Royal humility. Royal is already showing signs of privilege, expecting too much from life, just as Sheila used to.

She rises from the bench and heads back toward the path. Normally she walks around the lake at least once before going home. But the moon is barely a sliver tonight and the way is hard to see. She reaches for the pine straw of the path with her foot, her arms held out to the sides like a tightrope walker, embracing the empty air.

Fill In the Blank

1. If I were a bird, I'd be a_____.

Nighthawk, she writes. Not a hawk at all, but a gray and white bird ticked like a mattress. Nighthawks nested every spring on the edge of the driveway at home in shallow cups made of twigs and grass. When Garland approached, the parent birds danced away from the chicks, dragging an open wing. *Look at me! Take me!*

2. If I were a word, I'd be_____.

Surmise, because all of life is uncertain. Nothing to do with surprise, except for the rhyme, which you keep on hearing, like feeling your hat on your head after you've removed it.

3. If I were an object, I'd be a_____.

Without hesitation Garland writes *ring.* Round and perfect, like the pattern of the quilt her mother had made, "World-without-End." Interlocking rings that slipped in and out of each other. She'd be a ring pavéd with rubies, like the ruby slippers of her namesake, Judy Garland. And to match the stud in her navel, which was set in a gold circlet like a tiny pull-tab. Sometimes she imagined tugging it until she turned inside out—intestines, heart, and lungs blooming from her belly like slick flowers.

Since she was a child, Garland McKenney, aged twenty, has known that she would perish at a young age, like her mother, who died of a stroke at twenty-six while watching *Laugh In*. So inured is Garland to this belief that she hasn't the faintest awareness of it. She only knows she is hungry— for food, for sex, for risk—for life.

Not long after Garland arrived in New York City a year and a half ago she stopped telling people the name of her hometown. Instead, she simply said "Florida," and let them picture tourists gleaming with suntan oil and gold chains on the beaches of the south. The state might as well have ended at Disney World for all they knew about North Florida and a town like Sweetheart.

The first time she noticed Kroner's Physical Therapy she was temping at a brownstone next door. From her office window on the third floor she watched people limp in and out, including her boss, who had a slipped disk. Garland once delivered a contract to her while she lay under hot packs in a treatment room. Afterward, she had used the bathroom and noticed the closet with the door ajar and the purses hanging there like ripe fruit on a tree. That's when the idea first occurred to her.

Would anyone at Kroner's remember her from that one brief visit? Her hair had been long and brown then; now it was black, with dreadlocks accumulating like dust bunnies on either side of her face. The semihomeless look, her roommate,

Linda, called it. She'd met Linda at a Laundromat. On the day Garland moved in to Linda's tenement apartment on the Lower East Side, the two had celebrated by having their tongues pierced.

"All we need is an Ace bandage," Garland told Linda one evening, not long after she'd visited Kroner's. She wedged two pillows under her head on their shabby couch. "Beyond that, we'll play it by ear. We're just going to be using their bathroom."

"Do you think they'd let two complete strangers use the john? This is New York," Linda said.

Garland thought for a moment. "You have a point."

They decided to smoke a joint. Garland liked company when she got stoned. Alone, she became homesick. She never yearned for the people in Sweetheart, only the wildness of the place. She missed the kingfishers chittering as they swooped along the Sweetheart River, the deer grazing at night on the riverbank, their crystal-blue eyes bunched together like a chandelier.

Linda examined a strand of her streaky blond hair. "Have you ever done anything like this before?"

Garland couldn't decide how much to tell. She wanted Linda to have confidence in her plan, but she didn't want her to think she was a hardened criminal. "Let's just say I've broken the law more than once. What about you?"

"Me too." Linda giggled. "I've crossed the street on red. And I've shoplifted." She frowned. "A lot."

They compared what they'd shoplifted, and from which stores. Then Linda asked, "What else have you done?"

Garland's mind sorted through her transgressions, which she imagined as newspaper headlines: UNDERAGE GIRL BUYS BEER AT PIGGLY WIGGLY. TEEN GROWS MARIJUANA IN 4-H FIELD. JUVENILE DEFACES COURTHOUSE BATHROOM.

"Come on," Linda wheedled. "I thought we were sisters."

"We are, we are." Garland trusted Linda. Linda was generous, lent Garland clothes, money, jewelry, and makeup. Most of all, Linda was affectionate in a way that Garland had never encountered and found irresistible. Though Linda was straight and had a boyfriend, she held Garland's hand when they shopped, and put her arm around her on the street. When they watched TV together, she'd rest her head on Garland's shoulder. She was a tall, fleshy girl who kissed women as well as men on the mouth—wet kisses that were innocent and completely genuine. People felt loved by Linda. Once, early on, Garland had caught herself mimicking Linda's free and easy ways, and it had embarrassed her to realize how much she admired her new friend. She would have to wait until she lived somewhere else before she could adopt Linda's charms as her own.

Linda attached a hairpin to the joint, then tapped the ash.

"Did you grow up in Europe or something?" Garland asked. She had seen people kissing like Linda in European films.

"Me? Europe? Get out! You know I'm from Pennsylvania." Linda inhaled. "This is good weed. Come on"—she pressed through held breath—"tell me what crimes you've committed."

Garland told Linda about all her run-ins with the law as a

kid. While she talked, the two of them collected their perfumes onto a tray and took turns smelling them.

"Normal teenage stuff. But you got caught. I wonder why," Linda mused.

"I'd have to attribute it to native stupidity. Oh, and the expert guidance of my teachers and parent. Such shining examples of assholehood." The high school counselor had been wrong: she hadn't gotten caught to get attention since there were virtually no consequences. None of it had mattered. "Listen, I've got an idea." Garland sniffed from a squat bottle of L'Air Du Temps. "I'll go to Kroner's wearing the Ace bandage by myself a day or so beforehand and ask about physical therapy. Then we'll come back and do it."

"Yeah, then we'll clean them out," Linda added.

After that, they referred to the plan as a "cleaning job," as if they were after-hours maids. Neither of them ever said the word "robbery."

Garland unscrewed the cap on a tiny sample of White Shoulders, took a deep breath, and swooned on the cushions.

Linda bolted straight up. "We could buy an old car with the money, get out of the city on weekends. I could drive upstate instead of taking the bus or train." She sank back into the couch. "Or we could take a trip. I've never been to Mexico."

"We could." Leaning against Linda in a cloud of sumptuous aromas, Garland felt closer to her roommate than she had to anyone in a long time.

4. If wishes were rabbits, disappointments would be: (a) lions (b) hatboxes (c) frogs (d) rabbit-skin coats.

Garland had been subjected to all sorts of tests in her life—SATs, PSATs, an IQ test in seventh grade—but never one with such a bizarre question. Irrelevant, too: she didn't waste her time wishing for things. Her father, Eastman, wasn't the fairy godmother type. He'd granted only one wish in her life: Judy, the massive pit bull mix he rescued from the Tupelo County Animal Shelter for Garland's tenth birthday. Judy was a sweet but scary-looking dog, and people were leery of her. Garland took her along everywhere; it made her feel safer. When she became a dog-walker in New York City, Garland decided to specialize in large problem-dogs that other walkers rejected: Dobermans, pit bulls, shepherds, the big unruly mutts. Garland adored the dogs she walked; she was proud of reforming the recalcitrant barkers and nippers. Taking a cue from Linda, whenever she encountered clients walking their own dogs on the weekends, she'd kiss the dogs smack on the muzzle. The owners seemed mildly embarrassed by this outpouring of affection. She knew they pitied her for being one of those single women who had replaced people with animals, but they trusted her completely.

The idea of a rabbit-skin coat outraged her.

Later that week, Garland showed Linda pictures of Clarence, calling him her ex-flame. She didn't mention he was the Tupelo County sheriff.

"Manly." Linda touched the photo with her finger. "Nice torso."

"He's got really good legs, too, and a butt from heaven."

"I didn't know they gave out butts in heaven."

They were lying on their backs at opposite ends of the sofa, the soles of their feet pressed together. Linda raised up to pass Garland a joint. She held on to Garland's wrist, studying her green fingernails. "Cool polish," she whistled. "You're such a girlie girl."

"It's from all that Southern fried chicken."

"So why'd you break up with him?"

What Garland had loved most about Clarence was that he desired her in a way that compelled him to take chances. He was completely at the mercy of this profound lust—or was it love?—for her. For Clarence, the affair with Garland was the equivalent of cheating on the whole town. "Oh, he lied to me sometimes," she told Linda. "And we always had to sneak around to be together."

"Why?"

"He was married. When I got angry at him, he was afraid I'd tell his wife or blab it." Garland would never have used Clarence's wife against him, but after he mentioned it, she realized he didn't trust her not to.

"God," Linda said, closing her eyes. "You can't have a relationship if you can't get mad."

"Is this one of your yoga positions?" Garland asked, aware of pressure coming from the soles of Linda's bare feet.

"Yoga isn't done in pairs, you idiot." Linda laughed. "You know, I'd kill Kyle if we were married and he had a girlfriend. That's why I never want to get married. I'd be such a bitch."

"Really?" Garland had always admired the way Linda managed her relationship with Kyle, who lived upstate. Nothing rattled Linda. "You're usually so relaxed about Kyle."

"Oh, I am. Because we're not married."

"But you love him enough to marry him, don't you? What difference would a piece of paper make?"

"Worlds of difference, my dear," Linda said. "Worlds."

5. **When I'm angry, I: (a) tell people off (b) break things (c) cry (d) go shopping.**

As a kid, when Garland was upset she found solace in the family photo albums. Because she didn't remember her mother, who died when she was six, she'd spent hours poring over the professional portraits from the Sears in Tallahassee and candid snapshots captioned by her parents: *Garland at 22 mo. Lorelei and Garland swimming at Wakulla Springs.* Often, Lorelei and Garland wore identical mother-daughter outfits that Lorelei had sewn. She tried to love her mother as she turned the pages, but felt instead like a spy memorizing someone else's past.

Whenever Garland got into trouble, Eastman would invoke his dead wife, doubly aggrieved because she wasn't there to share his frustration. "My poor Lorelei," he'd say piously, hanging his head so his chin touched the second button on his shirt. "I'm glad she never lived to suffer this heartache." And, "If your mother wasn't already dead, this surely would kill her"—as if Garland's only role in life was to be the daughter of a dead woman.

Garland pitied her mother for dying young, but anyone could see that the real tragedy was Garland's: to be raised by

Eastman McKenney, the most boring, humorless man on Earth. The Human Dust Bowl. Mr. Zero—that's what his students called him when he taught math, before he became principal. Twenty years in high school had shaped him in peculiar ways. His daily life consisted of an inflexible collection of habits. He rose each morning at six forty-five, put on one of five suits, drank a cup of coffee, ate a bowl of grits into which he'd stirred two dabs of butter and a raw egg, then drove to work. Garland often had the sensation she was hearing his voice through a PA system. He behaved identically to everyone, as if he'd forgotten he ever had a private life.

If her mother had lived, maybe Eastman wouldn't have stiffened into a billboard of a person. At least Lorelei would have taught Garland to keep house. Carlene, the woman who cooked and cleaned for them, didn't mind if Garland never lifted a finger. She even picked up Garland's dirty clothes from the floor without a reprimand. Carlene had low expectations of white people. Inadvertently she had trained Garland to become a slob.

6. When I go to a party, I usually: (a) talk with people I know (b) talk with strangers (c) observe people (d) leave as soon as I can for one reason or another.

The only parties Garland knew much about were the private kind she and Clarence had had. In most of her recollections, they are sitting around in their underwear.

The following Tuesday afternoon, with Linda stationed at the corner, Garland rang the bell of Kroner's Physical Therapy, her arm snugged in an Ace bandage. She was clad in black, wearing sunglasses. Both girls had decided that Garland's hair was too distinctive, so she'd covered it with a knit cap.

She was buzzed through two electric doors to the waiting room. A plump, middle-aged receptionist talking on the phone motioned her to take a seat.

The room was dirty, with beige walls that hadn't been painted in an ice age and red carpeting so discolored by dark oily patches that Garland itched just looking at it. The motley assortment of furniture might have been salvaged from the street. She and Linda had filled their apartment with such discards. Curb foraging, Linda called it. If Garland had truly needed physical therapy, she wouldn't trust this place. A cheapskate—Mr. Kroner himself?—was clearly interested in separating people from their money first and foremost.

The receptionist hung up the phone. "How can I help you?"

"I've got tennis elbow, though I don't play. I thought I'd stop by, check out my insurance, maybe take the two-cent tour."

"Of course," the woman said. "My name is Grace."

"Virginia," Garland replied, shaking hands. "I work in the neighborhood."

"Where?"

"I just . . . babysit," she fluffed. "I'm in school. You know, college."

"Let me show you the facility." Grace pushed back her chair and squeezed past a dented filing cabinet. "What insurance do you have?"

"Cigna." Was that the name she'd seen on the subway ads?

"We take Cigna. I think you get twelve visits."

Garland followed Grace down a narrow hallway with four numbered rooms opening off it. In one, a patient lay under bulky towel packs. At the end of the hallway, Grace pointed out the bathroom. Next to it was the closet Garland had noticed on her earlier visit. Again, the door was ajar. At least six pocketbooks hung on hooks. She marked the spot on the mental map she was sketching. The hallway ended at a curtain, which Grace rattled aside on metal hooks to reveal a measly exercise room with a Nordic track, treadmill, and universal machine. The room was dingy, with a naked overhead bulb and a small ground-level window. No back door, Garland noted.

"Do you have the doctor's prescription for treatment? I could book your first appointment and start processing the paperwork," Grace said as they returned to the waiting area. She handed Garland a business card.

"I'm picking it up in a couple of days. I'll stop by after that."

Outside, Garland spotted Linda slouching at the corner, paging through *Vogue*. They hurried to the subway. "Way cool," Linda said, nestling her head on Garland's shoulder as Garland told her everything.

7. **If my father were a food, he'd be: (a) an omelet (b) a Popsicle (c) a steak (d) a cherry pie.**

She blacks out the choices and substitutes *celery*.

8. If my mother were a food, she'd be: (a) meatloaf (b) wine (c) macaroni and cheese (d) fish filet.

Even though most food is dead and my mother is dead, this is not relevant.

Friday was a good day for a robbery, Garland reasoned, because people were distracted. The caution with which they had armed themselves on Monday would have thinned to an impatience for the weekend to arrive.

Linda and Garland smoked a little dope to chill out before taking the train uptown. Dressed in nondescript wool slacks and a sweater, Garland was feeling confident. Linda, in denim, wore reflective sunglasses. Garland knew that behind them, Linda's eyes brimmed with excitement. Each girl carried an empty tote.

A baby on the floor of Kroner's waiting room was crawling across the stained red rug toward his mother, who was chatting on a cell phone. It made Garland sick to see the baby's nice clean body against the hairy, soiled floor. The baby put his fist in his mouth.

"Oh, hi," said Grace. "You're back."

"I'm ready to make my appointments. This is my friend," Garland said. "Allison, Grace."

"Hello," Linda said. She turned and whispered to Garland as Grace placed a clipboard and pen on the desk.

"Would you mind if I used the ladies' room first?" Garland asked. "If *we* used the restroom?"

Grace cast a sharp glance at the two young women. "It's at the end of the hall. Remember?"

Garland hooked pinkies with Linda, the thrill of trespass

surging through her body as they stepped down the hall. The layout matched the map she'd drawn for Linda. She could hear muffled voices behind two doors. The other two were open, revealing reclining figures engulfed in darkness. But there was a fifth door at the end of the corridor where she remembered none. A plate on it said OFFICE. How had she missed it?

They reached the bathroom. Beyond the curtain of the exercise room something metallic thunkety-thunked.

"Turns out I really do have to pee," Linda muttered, entering the single bathroom.

As before, the closet door stood open. Garland snatched a purse from a hook and quickly filched the wallet. She slipped it into her tote, then proceeded to the next purse and a third. Linda emerged, her face eager.

"Check the coat pockets," Garland whispered, then went into the bathroom and closed the door behind her. Two of them standing at the closet might arouse suspicion.

Garland looked at her watch. How long since they'd left Grace? She'd meant to note the time. She used the toilet, washed her hands, yanked a paper towel from the dispenser, and checked her watch again: twenty-two seconds had elapsed. She walked out of the bathroom.

Linda wasn't there.

A pile of coats littered the closet floor. She resisted the urge to hang them up.

A noise caught her attention. She stepped into the main hallway. Nothing. She peeked around the curtain of the exercise room. An elderly man was working weights on pulleys. He grunted and closed his eyes. He hadn't seen her.

Perhaps Grace had summoned Linda to the front. Garland craned her neck, but she was at the wrong angle to see the reception area. I am going to kill Linda, she thought.

A timer buzzed in one of the rooms. The office door swung open to reveal a lanky man with a pencil wedged behind his ear and a chart in his hand. Garland froze, a shower of icy needles bombarding her spine and chest. Pretending to retrieve something from the floor, she nudged the closet door shut. When she stood back up, the man was staring at her. "Can I help you?" Surprise and annoyance tinged his voice.

"Yes. Well, no. I'm just signing up for treatment." The voice sounded like pre–New York Garland, her old North Florida drawl bubbling up through her fear. "Grace let me use the john before I did my paperwork."

The timer continued to gnaw at the air.

"I'll get Mrs. Millstein off her electric stim," he shouted. A muffled female voice thanked him.

She hated this guy for making her feel like a schoolkid caught in the hall without a bathroom pass. She hated his crappy furniture and snot-colored walls. He was probably the son of a bitch who didn't care if babies had to crawl on filthy rugs.

"See you again soon," he said in a friendlier tone. "Oh, I'm Hank Kroner." He had a doughy face and trim body. About thirty-five, Garland guessed.

"Virginia." As Garland took his hand, she imagined the tote bag swinging forward of its own volition, dumping the stolen cache at his feet. She tried to hold his gaze, but he turned and strode into Room 3, chatting airily as the door clicked shut behind him.

The office door opened again and Linda burst through it. "Jackpot!" she squealed, her voice breaking. "Big jackpot!"

"Shut *up*!" Garland hissed.

Another buzzer sounded, and Grace appeared in the hallway, startled to see the two women there. A question formed on her face, but the buzzer prevented her from asking it. "I'm coming, Mr. Marx," she called, disappearing behind a door.

In the reception room, they stepped around the baby, who was now sitting upright, trying to wedge both fists in his mouth, his blue romper webbed with red lint. They bustled through the inner and outer doors, down the brownstone steps to the cold, sunny street. The abrupt change of light reminded Garland of leaving the Saturday matinee as a child, that moment she was spilled back into the daylight and realized, always with amazement, that the movie was the false world and this featureless, encompassing brightness the real one.

9. When my employer drops $100 under my desk, I decide to: (a) return it immediately (b) treat everyone in the office to lunch (c) return it later (d) spend it at the mall.

The money totaled $2,200, which they divided equally. Linda had found $1,410 in a strong box under Kroner's desk, where she had dived when he walked in. "My body felt like it was on fire," she told Garland. "I can't believe I did it. We're going to have some good shit to reminisce about when we're old and gray."

"Yep." Garland squared her stack of cash. "It'll always be a bond between us." Now she understood that Linda had come along not for twenty minutes of being thrillingly alive, but to fashion an adventure to paste into her memory book. She did it so she could say she had done it, so she could hark back to the experience, like looking at vacation pictures. It was probably the last illegal thing Linda would ever do. "Hey, do you know why Kroner had that stash hidden in his office?"

Linda looked at her blankly.

"He's skimming, pocketing cash off the top to avoid paying tax on it. No wonder he won't spring for decent carpeting." She'd learned about skimming from Clarence, who claimed everyone in business did it.

Linda said, "When my friend Roger, the night manager at Starbuck's, did that, they called it theft, but if you own your own business, it's skimming. It doesn't even sound illegal. It sounds like waterskiing." She dropped her money into a silk jewelry pouch. "The working class really does get screwed."

Garland punched her on the arm. "You're a regular Robin Hood."

"Do you want these?" Linda pushed a pile of misshapen wallets toward Garland. Without knowing what she would do with them, Garland dumped them into her dresser drawer.

On Sunday, Garland braved the tourists in SoHo to buy shoes at Tootsie Plohound—red leather pumps with round heels shaped like upside-down lighthouses. Back home she posed the pair stepping jauntily forward on her bureau so she could admire them from her bed.

She tossed the wallets onto her mother's "World-without-End" quilt, then, one by one, removed their contents, discarding the random bits of paper, and scissoring the credit cards to a jagged heap.

Her attention shifted to what remained: IDs and photos. These she arranged on the bed into family groupings, spinning stories about them the way she used to play with paper dolls. Fancily dressed children encircled a blue Christmas tree; a bar-mitzvah boy posed solemnly with his prayer shawl and yarmulke. Among the bouquets of faces, she identified the progenitors, their countenances like pressed corsages. She named them Lassiter, Cauthen, Ventadour. There were elders from Kansas, and European cousins thrice-removed wearing threadbare woolen jackets. Now the quilt resembled the family album that Lorelei had hoped to fill. There would be paternal aunts and uncles, and maternal ones. She shuffled a few pictures from one group to another. Here was a daughter who joined the air force, a distant cousin on Eastman's side serving time for embezzling, the twin nieces she'd never met on Lorelei's side who owned a dress shop in Atlanta.

Was it her imagination, or was Linda acting funny? Though Linda had described the robbery to Kyle on the phone, when he visited a week later, she forbade Garland to discuss it, claiming that it made her feel creepy.

"Creepy?" Garland echoed. She cut a BLT in half. The trio was preparing lunch in the tiny kitchen.

"It makes me nervous."

"You weren't nervous when we did it. I was the one who nearly peed in my pants when Kroner walked out of his office."

Kyle laughed.

"Stop it!" Linda said. "You're talking about it again."

Garland had complied. The rest of that day, Kyle and Linda stayed in Linda's bedroom, even for dinner. They spent Sunday at the Central Park Zoo, a place the three of them had frequented in the past. Kyle told her that he and Linda needed some time by themselves.

Kyle left at dawn on Monday. That afternoon, after work, Garland bought the ingredients for spaghetti with meatballs, Linda's favorite. While she cooked, Linda remained in her bedroom. She was unusually quiet during dinner.

"Is anything the matter?" Garland finally asked. It was just a formality—obviously something was wrong.

"Nope."

"You're acting strange."

"No, I'm not." Linda had wound so much pasta on her fork that it looked like a cone of cotton candy.

"You are. Are you mad at me?"

Sighing, Linda set the fork down. She regarded Garland, her face so sad it looked as if it would melt. "I feel guilty about what we did." Tears began to trickle down her cheeks.

Garland moved to Linda's side of the table and did what she imagined Linda would do: she draped her arms around her friend's neck and kissed her on the cheek. "Don't cry, baby. It's okay." She pushed back the hair on Linda's forehead. "Everything's over and you're safe."

"No, I'm not," Linda blubbered. "We could still get caught. I feel horrible, even if you don't."

"I think we should discuss this and then you'll see that everything is all right. Let's calm down. Let's smoke a little, okay?"

Linda agreed, sitting at the table like a zombie while Garland rolled a joint. They smoked in silence, waiting until time stretched out like an elastic band and they found themselves staring at nothing.

They roused themselves to pile the dirty dishes in the sink, then settled in the living room, at opposite ends of the sofa. They'd planned to paint the living room walls apricot, but they were still a dull eggshell.

"Every time I see you it reminds me. I know I shouldn't blame you, but it was your idea," Linda told Garland.

"You gladly participated."

Linda hugged a throw pillow to her chest. "Yeah, and now I regret it. We might have stolen money intended to feed a child."

"Don't be melodramatic. Nobody's life changes because their pocket gets picked."

"You don't know that."

"None of the wallets even had enough money for a month's rent. Remember, most of it was Kroner's. And he's a crook."

Linda stared at her lap. "I think we're very different people."

Garland's breath caught in her chest. She knew what "different" meant—that you weren't a person at all. "Actually, we have a lot in common. You stole before you met me, in case you forgot."

"I don't think we have the same values," Linda said.

Garland's face felt hot. Her tenth grade boyfriend, Darryl, had said something like that when he took back his friendship ring. The next thing Linda would say was that she didn't want to hang out together anymore.

Instead, Linda clasped her hands behind her head. "I've decided to give my share of the money to Habitat for Humanity," she announced. "Maybe you should do the same."

"You've got to be kidding. What about the car?"

"We don't need a car."

"Duh! That's clear. We both knew we'd just buy crap with the money." Garland tossed a pillow onto the floor and kicked it with her foot. Something shifted in her, as when an animal realizes the stick its owner is holding is intended for its head. She heard her own voice rise. "Now I think we *should* buy a car, to ease your conscience. We should buy a car and take poor kids for rides, what do you say?" That was weak. "You're so judgmental," Garland stumbled. "I thought you were special, but you're so ordinary. You're just like everyone else."

"Exactly," Linda said. "You're the one who's weird."

10. **Flower is to seed as _____ is to teenager: (a) education (b) adult (c) loneliness (d) driving.**

Though she knows there are no right answers on a test like this, that it is designed to reveal things about her, Garland ponders the analogy. She can make a case for any of the answers. If you love learning, then the flower of your life could be *education*. On the other hand, if you think misery is an innate part of growing up, you might pick *loneliness*. She wants to pick *loneliness*, but she worries it will make her seem pathetic, so instead she picks *adult*.

Linda wrote the check to Habitat for Humanity in front of Garland, sealing the envelope with a kiss.

In the next week, when they food-shopped, Linda used a separate cart. On the street, instead of holding hands, she skipped ahead or hung back, pretending to look at something on a tree or in the gutter. Garland wasn't fooled. In fact, she was touched by these awkward deceptions. They gave her hope. She didn't think Linda would go to the trouble of creating excuses for her behavior if she were planning on dumping her. Garland believed if she were patient, Linda would come around on her own. Besides, she thought Linda wanted to be left alone.

A few days later, Linda invited Garland into her room while she was packing for a long weekend at Kyle's. "I know you think I'm giving you the cold shoulder," Linda said, sitting down on the bed next to Garland.

"You're treating me like I have the plague," Garland whispered, on the verge of tears.

"I'm not trying to." Linda put her arm around Garland, lightly. "It's just happening. I can't help myself. And I know I'm just as guilty as you."

Garland had never known anyone to speak so honestly.

"I'm so sorry," Linda said. "I know it sucks for you."

It was as if a giant hand had reached down and seized Linda, leaving her dangling just out of reach. All Garland could do was watch as Linda twisted and turned, struggling to free herself.

Linda resumed packing, throwing socks into her bag.

"Do you want me to go with you to the Greyhound terminal?" Garland offered. It was nearly midnight and a light sleet was falling. Linda would be traveling most of the night to reach Kyle's town.

"No, I'll be all right."

"I'll bet you wish you had that car now."

Linda zipped up her suitcase. "How can you joke about it?"

"Aw, come on, Linda. I'm not allowed to crack a joke?"

"I guess not." Linda frowned, then turned and looked straight at Garland. "What I really wish is that I could confess, take my medicine, and be done with it."

"Don't say that, okay?" Garland felt the blood draining out of her face. "Not even as a joke. It really freaks me out."

"Sorry." Linda walked toward the front door with Garland following. She donned her coat in silence.

"I'm sorry, too, okay?" Garland's tears welled up at last. "But I can't undo it. You're just going to have to forgive yourself." *And me,* she wanted to add, but didn't. She wanted to comfort Linda and have Linda comfort her in return. She wanted them to dissolve into laughter and fall into each other's laps the way they used to. Instead, Linda bustled down the narrow hallway, mumbled good-bye, and slammed the door without once turning around.

Three days later, Kyle and Linda phoned. Kyle explained that he'd be spending more time in the city, staying in the apartment with Linda. In mild, hollow voices the pair asked Garland to find a new place to live. Though Garland knew this was a lie intended to spare her feelings and avoid a scene, she couldn't muster even an iota of rage. She felt crushed.

Because she hadn't bought anything with the robbery money but the shoes, Garland had no difficulty producing the security deposit and last month's rent for a studio sublet in less trendy Murray Hill.

Her view of New York from the eighteenth floor reduced the city to a more manageable grid devoid of individual faces. A mirrored alcove next to her bedroom glittered with designer lipsticks and nail polish boosted from the best department stores. She had added three rottweilers to her daily roster and begun boarding dogs in her apartment at exorbitant prices. Her roommates were all canines, she joked to herself. New York was starting to feel like home.

One evening two months later, Garland recognized Linda's number flashing on her caller ID. They hadn't spoken since Garland moved out. Garland had dealt with the pain of the broken friendship by staying busy and putting Linda out of her mind. What good could come from speaking now, when she was just getting used to her life without Linda?

"Hello, Linda," she said, snatching up the receiver on the last ring.

"Caller ID, huh? Or are you psychic?"

"Both. What are you up to?"

"Oh, the usual. What about you?"

"Yeah, the usual." Garland waited, letting the chilly silence accumulate, like snow.

Finally, her voice shaking, Linda said, "I have something to tell you." Words that always heralded tragedy—a traffic accident, dying parent, pregnancy?

Garland waited again.

"I'm going to the police tomorrow." Linda's voice dropped. "To confess. I just wanted to give you a heads-up."

Garland felt woozy.

"I don't expect you to understand, but it hurts me. Every day I feel worse and worse. I'm sick to my stomach. I can't eat, I can't sleep. I've got to get some relief."

"Have you considered Valium?"

"Can you ever be serious?"

"I am serious. Come on, Linda, please don't rat me out." She hated the pleading tone in her voice.

"Garland, listen, I have a lawyer, and he says if we confess together, we'll get probation. He's willing to represent both of us."

"I thought we were straight on this. I mean, shit, I moved out like you wanted."

"I'll go crazy if I don't do it. I already feel crazy."

"Have you ever heard of loyalty?" She had believed that Linda loved her, Linda understood her.

"I'm sorry. I don't blame you anymore. I've been seeing a shrink, and now the lawyer. It's tomorrow at ten-thirty. Please come."

Garland's mind felt like the room in the Edgar Allan Poe story in which the walls begin to contract. She couldn't breathe. "What's the lawyer's name and address?" Sighing, she grabbed a ballpoint pen and scrawled the information on her forearm. "I'll think it over," she said, and hung up.

Garland sat without moving for a long time, her breathing deep and slow, as if she were nodding off. Her juvenile records in Sweetheart had been sealed; they couldn't be used against her. Clarence had never reported what she'd done for fear of being compromised himself. His angry face surfaced in her memory, red as a boiled crab.

Garland had started breaking rules at such a young age that she couldn't recall if she had ever felt like confessing. She didn't think so. Linda, however, stewing in her apartment, was another case altogether. Apparently, for Linda the desire had erupted and spread like a bodily contagion.

Mr. Michelson was a white-haired man with small, watery eyes and a kindly expression. He greeted the two young women warmly, directing them to thick leather chairs angled casually toward his desk. The office had a homey look that probably translated to a high bill. Garland hoped Mr. Michelson would accept a postdated check. She had $230 to her name, not counting credit cards.

She listened as he summarized what had happened, how Linda had phoned him, crying. He stressed how pleased he was that she had come forward, and now Garland. First-timers, he said, worried about two things: getting caught and being forgiven. Confession was the remedy for both. In the end, the girls would be happy with their decision. His voice was even and reassuring. He'd arranged a brief interview with the captain at the local precinct where they would be booked.

Garland had not realized how much she had missed Linda until she saw her in the lawyer's waiting room. Linda had stood and embraced her, then quickly returned to *Entertainment Weekly*. She still had not spoken to Garland, and now she avoided looking at her. Gone for good, Garland thought with a pang. In the past, she'd felt justified when she made other people suffer. Now, she wondered: did her regret for losing Linda count as genuine remorse, or was it more selfishness?

They would be arrested, photographed, fingerprinted, and then sent home. The police captain, he said, was a sympathetic guy with kids of his own.

Linda had been sniffling from the first moment, but Garland remained dry-eyed. As the lawyer talked, she realized that she was beginning to feel better, as if she had eaten a solid meal and was now settling down to a good video. It seemed impossible, considering that he was now discussing bail bonds. She felt optimistic, as if she were anticipating something beyond the punishment. But what?

Since they were pleading guilty, there would be no jury. "That's good," the lawyer continued. "I hate to rely on juries. Some of them are prejudiced toward single young women. If you came into court with a baby stroller, that would be one thing. But you girls . . ." He smiled at each of them in turn. "You look like you're having too much fun. A jury might imagine lying awake at three in the morning, worried out of their skulls about you."

Garland said, "You mean we look like troublemakers?"

"If you dress the way I tell you, the judge won't take you for a troublemaker."

"Are we dressed all right now, for the police station?" Linda asked.

"You're fine," the lawyer said. "Do you have any other questions?"

Garland felt sorry for Linda, worrying about dressing respectably. Undoubtedly this was a girl who would never jaywalk again. Garland, on the other hand, was feeling less frightened. The calm that had surfaced moments before now settled around her like a soft old blanket. "What's actually going to happen to us?" she asked.

"You're first offenders, so the law will go easy on you." He explained that they'd be sentenced and then, most likely, given probation for a couple of years, assigned community service or counseling or both. They'd have to allocute to the crime, to tell the details to the judge. That would be the most humiliating part, he said.

Linda burst into tears. Mr. Michelson whisked out a tissue, passed it to her, and continued. "You should think of community service as a job you can never be absent from. If you are, they can throw you in jail."

"I'm not really scared," Garland blurted. "I guess I feel relieved."

"But you're the one who didn't want to do this," Linda objected angrily through her tissue. "You should be glad that I called you."

Garland knew that Linda expected gratitude, that she had a right to it, but she could not bring herself to thank her.

———

Garland had rarely asked herself why she kept breaking rules. When she did wonder, when she closed her eyes and concentrated, she had always envisioned the same thing: herself in a car, careening along a curving mountain road. In this waking dream, the robbery or graffiti or arson was neither her destination nor the place she was hurrying from. It was another tap on the gas pedal.

But now that she had been caught, the girl in the fast car paused ever so slightly to look back and glimpse the wreckage in her wake: Linda weeping, endlessly weeping, a crowd of indistinct others congregated behind her.

———

Four months later, in a trial that took less than twenty minutes, they were sentenced to community service. Garland, the admitted instigator, was also ordered to attend counseling, where each week the feeling of being caught reasserted itself, producing an odd joy. You might have thought she had fallen in love.

In early May the parks of New York City bulged with people. Especially noticeable were those whom illness or age had confined all winter—the elderly with walkers; those gone bald and fragile from chemotherapy; people rolling by in wheelchairs. The parks ran with torrents of baby squirrels and children pursued by clamoring nannies. Frisbees and baseballs soared over the paths and promenades through air tinted lime green by the new spring scrim of leaves.

Garland sat on a bench beneath tall sycamores, contemplating faces from every continent. She'd once told Linda that the only things Sweetheart and New York had in common were the sky and the asphalt. The faces of Sweethearts were sunburned and etched with deep lines from a life lived out of doors on tractors, in boats, and, in backyards. New Yorkers' faces were blander, blanker, more like masks. Subway faces, Linda had called them.

11. You will have a good life if you have: (a) sufficient money (b) a loving family (c) a good job (d) beauty.

Another tricky question. Is one of the four so powerful it could compensate for the other three? *A loving family?* Too sentimental, she decides, pure pap. *Beauty?* It can't be beauty. Most people will never be beautiful no matter how much weight they lose or what shampoo they use. *Money?* Well, money is crucial. But she's heard too many bitter stories of people who are rich and miserable, either because the money led them astray or because wealth wasn't good company on a cold night. *A good job?* No, no guarantee of happiness. Just look at Eastman: he loves his work and hates his life.

Her pencil hovers over the choices.

A loving family? She can only imagine what that is like. Or can she?

"Your time is up," her counselor announces. The voice is firm but kind, with a sustain like an organ note.

Garland leans back in her chair and places the number-two pencil on top of the test booklet. Maybe *that* was the key. If you never had it, could you imagine it?

Tourist Season

When her husband, Milt, retired, it was as if a bell that Frieda had heard ringing pleasantly in the distance all her life began striking right next to her head. Milt was everywhere she turned. "We're on our second honeymoon," he'd say, jollying her into another game of bingo, another round of golf. After four months of solid togetherness, while she was lying on the wicker settee on the balcony, Frieda daydreamed that Milt had dropped dead. Tears sprang to her eyes as she pictured him laid out in a casket, looking perfectly healthy. Deeply ashamed of her thoughts, she began to ponder ways for him to spend his time.

Nearly a decade before, Milt had bought a piece of a middleweight. It had been one of the most exciting times of his life—the domed dark of the armories, blue pillars of cigarette smoke, Milt hanging on the ropes, barking instructions to "the Hurricane." Frieda had loved it, too—loved the fighter's pink satin robe draped over the corner stanchion, voluptuous as the lip of a conch shell, loved the blowzy crowd and oily-faced vendors hawking drinks and programs. But Tadeusz

Simkowicz turned out to be a bleeder and after five bouts traded his Everlast shorts for a job selling Cadillacs.

What about investing in another fighter, Frieda suggested now.

No, Milt said. The fight game had lost its dignity. It was becoming a spectacle, like wrestling, the men wearing sequinned shorts and tutus, messages shaved into their hair.

Next, Frieda urged him to get involved in the management of their condo, maybe run for a seat on the board of directors.

No, definitely not for him. How could she suggest it? The directors were a bunch of bullies who couldn't pass for businesspeople if they had ticker tape coming out of their butts. He hated the officious notices they tacked on the bulletin boards. *There will be a ballot in your mailbox regarding pool chemicals (chlorine versus bromine). Vote by July 15 or lose your say in this important matter!!* Milt had sold tractors to Mexico and drilling equipment to Venezuela. He'd propped up dictators in Latin America with customs bribes. He wasn't about to waste his time debating whether to paint the lobby yellow or green. He was retired, goddammit, and he was going to do nothing with the rest of his life if he felt like it.

Then the Knoblocks, a couple who lived on their floor, split up after six months of fierce bickering. It seemed insane to Frieda at the time. But Gertie Knoblock wasn't budging. She had a lawyer. It was war now. All because they got on each other's nerves after retirement and had nothing—no children living nearby, no joint projects or family business—that required them to get along. Everyone in the building marveled at the irony of this tsouris: now that the Knoblocks could afford a deluxe condo on the Intracoastal Waterway, lacquered teak furniture, and Italian marble floors you could see your reflection in—PS, they could also afford a divorce.

Frieda took it as a cautionary tale and signed up to be a Pink Angel at the Santa Rosa Hospital. Five mornings a week, wearing a pink duck blazer with the word VOLUNTEER embroidered in red above the breast pocket, she chatted with patients, delivered mail, and arranged movie rentals.

———

Frieda put on her glasses to get her lipstick straight, dropped the tube into her purse, and jangled the car keys. "I'm going," she called to Milt, who was sitting at the breakfast table with three different newspapers spread out before him, as if he were compiling a concordance of the day's news. It took him a good two hours to read them all.

"Wait." He walked to the door and touched Frieda's wiry gray hair. They puckered at each other in the air.

It was eight-fifteen A.M. The women of Bluepoint Towers were already busy in the ninth-floor laundry room. Frieda could just make out their chatter and the labored spin cycle of the washer as she walked toward the elevator. When the doors parted, a man with a Polaroid camera suspended from his neck was standing inside, his eyes darting back and forth, his mouth nervously mobile. "Good morning," she said.

"My name, what's my name?"

Frieda held the doors open. "You're my neighbor, Irv Snyder."

"Oh, sure, I didn't actually forget it."

Frieda took him by the arm. "I'll take you back to your apartment, okay?"

"Fine. That's where I was going."

But Frieda knew it wasn't where he was going. She studied his grizzled, distinguished face: the robust eighty-two-year-old could have been an ancient Greek oracle. In fact, Irving Snyder suffered memory lapses. He drifted in and out of his life, the way the sun broke through cloud cover over Florida's Gold Coast. Sometimes he sat for hours in the recreation room, staring at the saloon-style gold-and-black flocked wallpaper while his wife and neighbors played card games and billiards. Other times, under his wife's watchful eye, he'd pace the perimeter of the shuffleboard court, or pick his way along the wooden promenade of the dock, taking snapshots with his Polaroid as if he hoped to find himself in the images that bloomed on the glossy paper.

"You know, Frieda, I've got all my own teeth." He smiled at her, revealing brown stubs like the ruins of a fort. "No choppers in a jar by the bed for me."

Belle Snyder opened the door of 908. "You've been gallivanting again?" she asked, her hands on her hips. "I turn my back for a minute to go to the bathroom and you're off, like Marco Polo?" She gave Frieda a knowing look and shook her head. "Irving, I'm going to get a leash for you if you keep leaving the apartment by yourself. A leash, like a dog."

Back in the elevator, Frieda's eye caught a flyer taped to the back wall: *Last date to sign up for the bus trip to St. Augustine is October 15. Be there or be square!*

On her way through the parking lot, Frieda thought of an-

imals finding their way home over hundreds of miles of foreign terrain. Spawning salmon. Migrating birds. Whales.
Heroic dogs like Lassie and Rin Tin Tin. For a brief moment
she imagined that Irv Snyder was one of those noble creatures,
following some instinctual path to his real life, where a house
and his youth and people long dead awaited him, their arms
extended in welcome.

Hallandale Beach Boulevard was clogged with cars as it was
most mornings during the tourist season, which stretched
from Thanksgiving to Easter and seemed to get longer each
year. Frieda waited at a traffic signal, watching a helicopter
hover above Interstate 95. The morning light glinted off its
fuselage, creating a fierce shock of radiance, like a second sun.

In May 1941, Frieda had been working in the millinery department of Rich's Department Store when Jacqueline
Cochran, the famous aviatrix, flew into town to promote her
line of cosmetics. Frieda bought a bottle of Pursuit perfume
(named for a kind of plane, she later found out). The next day,
she signed up for flying lessons. Within a year, the country
was at war and Frieda was flying for the Women's Airforce
Service Pilots.

After the war, the airlines wanted women stewards, not
women pilots. Her wings clipped, she married Milt, worked
part-time with him in his export business, and raised three
sons. At age sixty-five, she took retirement. Milt was still working then, and she found she enjoyed being alone. She began
keeping a journal and took community education courses in

art history. She even went to Greece without Milt for ten days. The trip was wonderful and so was their reunion when she returned.

———

At the hospital, the floor nurse asked Frieda if she knew a Janet Duquesne. "She's from your building," she explained. "A snowbird from Toronto. Just moved here. Heart palpitations. Her husband died four months ago."

"I don't know her." Frieda was relieved and then stricken with guilt. How could she entertain thoughts about avoiding Milt? She was lucky to have a husband—especially a *first* and only husband—still living. Most of the women she knew were widows with no reason to pluck the bristles from their chins. They went everywhere in committee-sized clutches, as if lifted from a PTA meeting in the fifties and transported through time, set down fingering nightgowns in Loehmann's Plaza, chattering over mah-jongg, eating the early-bird special at the Sun Ho restaurant. "I'll take her outside for lunch," Frieda said.

At eleven-thirty, the sky was a flat, Dutch blue. Perfect flying weather. Frieda hadn't soloed in the five years since her pacemaker was installed.

She parked Mrs. Duquesne in a patch of sun, opened her utensil package, and began the soothing small talk she had easily produced all her life. It flowed out of her automatically, the way a snail laid down its own slippery, protective runway. Mrs. Duquesne looked cheered by the end of lunch.

When she returned home at one P.M., Milt was waiting for her in his swim trunks, with towels, sunscreen, and hats neatly packed in a beach bag. Two tuna fish sandwiches faced each other on the kitchen table like duelists. "I figured we'd eat, then head for the beach," he said.

Frieda studied the sandwiches—bulging half-moons of rye bread, with frilly red lettuce sticking out like a flamenco skirt. "I'm tired," she said.

"Well, then, sweetheart, you can nap on the beach. You love the beach. You've always loved the beach."

"I just don't feel like going."

"Then I won't, either. We can go tomorrow."

"No, Milt, I don't want to promise that I'll go tomorrow." She pushed the plate of food away. "I married you for better or for worse." Her eyes filled up with tears. "But not for *lunch*."

They spent the rest of that afternoon in silence, watering plants, snoozing on the balcony, waiting for the evening news.

After dinner, Frieda mentioned the trip to St. Augustine. They hadn't been there for thirty years, when it was a nickel-and-dime tourist trap with a musty one-room log school-house. She showed Milt a brochure entitled "Florida's First Coast." Houses with walled gardens, cobblestone streets, and an old fort traversed its folds in splashes of color. "It's been re-stored," Frieda said. "You won't have to drive. 'The bus is air-conditioned, the seats recline,' " she read aloud, hurrying to quash objections before Milt could voice them.

"You want to be trapped for two days with all the old farts from this building?" Milt said.

Frieda dropped her eyes and gathered her patience. "The bus only holds forty-two old farts."

He glared at her.

"Look," Frieda said, "we've had this picture-postcard condo life for eight months, and we never budge out of it. We should take advantage of the group activities."

"You know I'm not a group activities kind of person. You do know that, don't you? A man who ran his own business for forty years—"

"I want to go on this trip," Frieda said. "If you don't go with me—"

"OK."

"And no complaining. I don't want to hear one complaint from you, at least not until it's over."

"All right. Sold. Golden years," Milt muttered. "They ought to call them gold-plated years."

Inside, she was twenty. She was twenty in her passion about landfills, African desertification, dolphins, the shrinking gene pool of food grains, the world her grandchildren would inherit. In her water aerobics class she *felt* twenty. There, three afternoons a week, nearly weightless in her foam Aquajogger belt, she floated standing up in the deep end and ran and ran, the jewel-clear turquoise water spreading out in ripples around her, like applause.

But Milt wasn't twenty or thirty. He was seventy-two. Not

because he took beta-blockers and his knees were gone and he could turn his neck in only one direction. But because out of the blue he'd say things like, "The ambulance will be coming for me one of these nights." The ambulance, a frequent visitor, always drew a crowd. Frieda hated the way its red lights reflected on the fountain in front of the lobby, turning the spray blood-red, like some Old Testament plague. "My luck," Milt would continue, "I'll tell them my symptoms, but the paramedics'll be Cuban or Haitian, God bless them. They won't understand a word I'm mumbling. Just another DOA."

———

The charter bus was a glossy cordovan color, like an expensive shoe. They loaded their suitcases in the cavity at the bottom and took their seats. The view was good so high up—more treetops and sky, less asphalt and metal. Gertie Knoblock, already aligned with the widows, played Tinkle on a lap desk at the back of the bus. Irving and Belle Snyder walked arm-in-arm, like young lovers, when the bus stopped at an outlet store selling flimsy towels and paperweights with flamingos that rained down glitter instead of snow.

The trip took seven hours. Milt and Frieda had each brought books. Milt read about Jewish prizefighters—Slapsie Maxie Rosenbloom, Barney Ross, and a few dozen others. He was always reading about Jews—Jews in Hollywood and the actors to whom they assigned gentile names; Jewish settlers in nineteenth-century Florida; Jewish painters; Ethiopian, Turkish, and Chinese Jews. It was Milt's way of *being* a Jew, Frieda had concluded, since he never went to temple. Frieda read a book on harems and was surprised to learn there really was a white slave trade.

"Look at that!" Milt pointed to a billboard welcoming them to FLORIDA'S FIRST COAST. On it, Spanish sailors with plumed hats kissed the earth. "What a great promotion. I mean, here we are, a stone's throw from Georgia where it actually snows," Milt clucked, "but we've got Florida *history* instead of Florida heat. And"—he pointed again—"some midget palm trees so it still looks tropical."

Frieda was happy to see him so animated. He had talked a blue streak before his retirement. As a salesman, he could talk anybody into anything, and though there were times when Frieda wanted somebody more like Gary Cooper, somebody more like a sculpture of a man whose iron features stood for all he need not say, she knew that talkers made better husbands. They gave you something to work with, so you weren't battling silence, empty space.

Frieda wasn't much of a talker. She was a doer. When the boys were little, some evenings she'd leave Milt at home and rent a Piper Cub. At 5,000 feet, the twinkling city and sky seemed mirror images of each other instead of places separated by vast, unimaginable distances. At home, when she climbed into bed, she imagined herself sleeping among stars.

Late afternoon sun fell through the trees and across the buildings of St. Augustine in great transparent golden bands. The bus driver circled around the Plaza, then dropped them at Malone's Bed-and-Breakfast, a Victorian mansion overlooking the inlet. Frieda and Milt ascended to the third floor in an old-style cage elevator. Their room was furnished with a high bedstead, *Gone with the Wind* lamps, and hooked rugs. A carved walnut wardrobe stood in the corner like a gigantic book. Milt climbed the bed ladder and bounced onto the mattress. "It's like a trampoline," he cried. Frieda joined him and lay back on the bed, beneath a canopy made of baby blue taffeta, like a shiny dome of sky. They kissed, Milt thrusting his tongue deep into her mouth. The first time they had kissed like that it was against regulations. Milt had been an aviation mechanic, and she was a pilot at a base nicknamed "Cochran's Convent."

She had walked differently in her flight suit. She swaggered, by God. Climb into the cockpit, secure the latch. Inside, the lights and gauges of the instrument panel waited like a small universe with its celestial clockworks exposed. She loved the feel of the stick in her hand when the great sheath of metal lifted into the endless Texas sky above Avenger Field, the roar of the engine so loud it became a kind of silence. Twenty thousand feet, breathing through the mask, the sun just a traffic light stuck on yellow as she rose above it.

—

Dinner on your own, said the brochure.

"Let's eat with Belle and Irv," Frieda offered. They knew Belle and Irv better than anyone else. And Frieda was drawn to them, as though she could prepare for her or Milt's senility by witnessing Irv's.

"Mr. Half-life," Milt snorted. "I mean, the guy's decaying right before our eyes. I'd rather eat alone."

That night, because, he said, the bed was so high off the

ground, Milt slept entwined around her, one leg between her knees like an anchor.

———

Frieda lay on the hard-packed sand near the tidal edge, which was still damp and cool from the night before. Behind her, on the sugary white dunes, teenagers sunbathed on the hoods of their cars, their radios blaring. Frieda thought it barbaric to allow cars on the beach, but according to the brochure, it was a time-honored tradition on the First Coast.

In the sunny breakfast room at Malone's, Frieda and Milt had decided to go to the beach before sightseeing. Belle and Irv Snyder had invited themselves along. Now Belle appeared, clutching the waistband of Irv's swimming trunks, steering him.

The Boogie boards Milt had rented brought him and Frieda gliding to shore, happy beached whales. Milt looked rugged and determined as he leaned into the surf, carrying the big blue hunk of plastic. Irv and Belle, too frail for the thrashing surf, stretched out on a beach blanket. In a few minutes, though, Irv was standing, his Polaroid around his neck. He began taking pictures of people at the beach, mostly pretty young girls in skimpy suits. Frieda heard him ask them to pose for him. "I'm a tourist," he said, again and again. "Would you mind if I took your picture to show my grandchildren up north?"

Milt wanted to Boogie board until it was time to leave, and for the first time in months, he didn't ask Frieda to join him. She donned her sunglasses and lay back, studying the white wisps in the sky, a biplane trailing a commercial message: EAT AT THE DIXIE CAB COMPANY.

I'm over the target now, she used to radio to ordnance. She had felt bloodlust as she crisscrossed the gunnery range going off like sparklers beneath her, firing at the target she towed behind her plane.

Just last year, Frieda had been interviewed for a book about the women pilots. Asked to describe her most unusual experience, Frieda told how she had once lost her bearings over the ocean, past the Outer Banks. When she finally came in late and low over the gunnery range, the cable operator was slow letting out the muslin target sleeve. It was only 100 instead of 300 feet behind her when live ammunition began to blister through the air. She gained altitude rapidly, but not before her Douglas Dauntless was riddled with holes. That night in her billet, she'd lain awake for hours, hearing the metal of the fuselage rip. One round had missed her by less than six inches. Ordnance said she was a hero. They apologized for the mistake, though, of course, the mistake had been hers. But wouldn't their spotlights have illuminated her plane as well as the target? For months afterward she broke out in a cold sweat at odd moments.

When the book came out, her story wasn't in it.

———

"Ripley's Believe It or Not Museum," Frieda said. "That's where I'm going first." She put a check mark beside the name in the *AAA Guide Book to Florida.*

"You're not taking the tram tour?" Milt's face crumpled.

Frieda quickly propped him up. "Why don't you come with me? The walking will do us both good. Besides, the tram doesn't stop long enough at any one place to really see it."

Milt did the math—two hours divided by fifteen: only four minutes per attraction. "All right, we'll go to Ripley's. But I want to see the fort. They kept Geronimo in the dungeons there, you know."

—

At Ripley's they saw an entire oil painting on the head of a pin, a two-headed calf, other freaks of nature, and hundreds of the original cartoons that ran in newspapers illustrating the odd facts Robert Leroy Ripley was so fond of collecting. An exhibit on Eng and Chang, the original Siamese twins, filled a whole room. Frieda and Milt stood silently absorbing the information about the twins' odd, conjoined lives. A series of photographs spanning four decades showed them at work at the circus and relaxing at home. They had each married and had nineteen children between them. They spent half their time in one household, half in the other. Frieda tried to imagine their sex lives, one negating himself, disappearing into a private void while the other pushed and grunted toward orgasm. She read on. When one died, the other died within hours—of fright, it turned out. There was a picture of the dead twins curled in their custom-made funeral suit like a dead spider. In a caption below, the doctor who performed the autopsy said that they could easily have been separated, that all that held them together was a thick muscular ligament at the breastbone.

"I bet they knew they could be separated all along," Milt said. "I bet they chose to stay attached for the money."

"I wonder," Frieda said. Maybe they were so used to being a creature with four arms and legs and two heads that separation would be a terrifying loss, like an amputation.

Milt took Frieda's hand as they exited into the bright sunshine and began walking toward the fort. There was a breeze so balmy, so oily with traffic exhaust and suntan lotion that Frieda felt the skin all over her body, felt where she stopped and the world began.

A crowd was gathering on the grassy mall that ran down to the bay. Frieda picked out the voice of Belle Snyder shrieking, "Help him! Somebody help him!"

Frieda and Milt walked faster and faster, until they were jogging toward the scene, despite Milt's bad knees and Frieda's irregular heart.

"Is anyone here a doctor?" Frieda called out. She elbowed her way through the throng, took Belle's hand, and repeated her question. Everyone looked down, ashamed they could do nothing but gawk and tsk at the tragedy before them. There on the ground lay Irv Snyder. People had backed off to give him air, so that he was encircled by a nimbus of grass, like a descending archangel in an old religious painting.

"All right." Frieda stepped into the cleared space. "You there." She singled out a young man in a khaki jumpsuit. "Call 9-1-1. Just walk over to that T-shirt store." She pointed across the street. Her mind was racing. It hadn't run this fast since she worked with Milt. No—since her WASP days.

Irv looked fragile, as if all the bones in his body might have snapped at once. He was nattily dressed for dinner in a pink shirt and white tie. A madras suit jacket lay bunched under one shoulder. "Oh my God, my God," Belle sobbed. "Somebody help him. Help him." Frieda knelt and put her fingers on Irv's neck to find a pulse. "His heart's beating," she announced. Probably had a stroke, she thought. Probably won't ever talk or walk again. Milt leaned down and gently loosened Irv's tie. The crowd watched in respectful silence.

Belle was leaning over Irv, wringing her hands. "We were walking through the castle, and I turned around, and he was gone. Poof! Just like that." She snapped her fingers. "Gone for a good half hour. I just now found him."

As Milt dislodged Irv's jacket, a bundle of pictures fell onto the grass. His Polaroids. But they were not of the girls at the beach or Bluepoint Towers or boats on the Intracoastal. At first, Frieda saw only that there was flesh—breasts and buttocks. Belle's breasts and buttocks. Belle with a large vibrator inside her. Belle on her knees, spreading her buttocks for a close-up of her anus, Belle pushing her breasts together, making the nipples touch like two giant crossed eyes. The crowd turned its attention from Irv to the photographs being passed eagerly from hand to hand. Frieda heard a succession of clicks and whistles, oohs and aahs.

Just then a boy of about sixteen pedaled by, saw the figure on the ground, threw his bike down, and rushed to Irv's side. "I know CPR," he exclaimed. He began thumping on Irv's chest, blowing into his mouth. As if on cue, Irv opened his eyes, bits of blue that matched the sky.

"Oh my God," Frieda said. "I bet he was just asleep."

That is the first thing you do, she remembered now from her CPR course: scream at the patient, slap him, if necessary, to make sure he isn't just dozing.

The boy continued: fifteen thumps on the sternal notch, then mouth to mouth. Irv raised up on one elbow. "Why is this beautiful boy kissing me?" he asked, smiling.

The ambulance arrived. Medics took Irv's vital signs and questioned him. Irv stood and stretched. He refused to go to the hospital.

Sleeping on the manicured lawn of the Plaza de la Constitución was not so unusual, it turned out. "Most of the time it's bums we get," the head medic explained. "Around December, January, they start flocking here, like birds on the flyway. But your guy's okay. Just take him home and let him finish his nap."

"He'll want his pictures back," Belle whispered to Frieda. "They're important to him."

Intent on the photos, the crowd hadn't dissipated. Frieda retrieved as many snapshots as she could and stuffed them in Belle's handbag.

"I did it to please him," Belle said. "He couldn't do anything but look anymore."

———

The Columbus Restaurant was a shrine to Spanish ornament. Frieda found the profusion of patterns and colors nauseating. Even the food was decorated with flower petals and bits of toxic greenery, each plateful as busy as a crazy quilt. She closed her eyes and saw Irv stretched out on the grass, the peaceful expression on his face before he was awakened. A line from an old poem about a dead lamb left out for crows to eat pulled across her mind like a banner: *The sleep looked deep.* At the edge of her consciousness she overhead Belle recounting Irv's story at a nearby table.

The early-bird special that evening was Florida lobster. Most of the diners wore lobster bibs with pictures of conquistadors on them. Milt never ordered specials. He liked to pay full price—for steaks, suits, cars, ties. It made him feel better, he said, than buying things on sale. As the waitress leaned down to tie a bib around his neck, he blurted out, "Are you going to bring me a high chair, too?"

"Excuse me?"

Milt turned to Frieda. "You might as well shoot me if you ever find me wearing a bib, with butter smeared all over my face and my hair sticking straight up."

"Pardon us for a moment, please," Frieda said to the waitress.

"I'd rather be dead than have you see me like that."

Frieda stood and grabbed Milt's elbow and marched him out of the restaurant. They walked to a hole-in-the-wall pizzeria two doors down and took a booth. Frieda scanned the laminated menu and ordered the "Lollapalooza." They sat in silence until Frieda could see that Milt was completely overcome with self-pity. "So you want me to remember you the way you were at age forty? Sixty? Thirty? You're a human being, not a photograph."

"A human being," Milt repeated.

The pizza arrived. Milt reached across the table, dug his

fingers into Frieda's arm, and began to weep. The waiter scurried away. "I only feel like a human being when I'm with you."

"That's ridiculous," Frieda said, patting his cheek, mopping a tear with her thumb. "A lot of people need and love you."

"I'm at the mercy of bellboys and waitresses. Ten-year-olds on skateboards feel free to give *me* the finger." He wiped his eyes and blew his nose. Then he served each of them a slice of pizza and stared past Frieda through a bright square of window. "You know, I think I miss having people to boss around."

Frieda waited a moment before she answered. "I think that's it. And you know what, Milt? You've been bossing me around instead."

"I've been bossing you around? Since when?"

"Since you retired. And sometimes before that, especially when the boys were little."

All at once their shared past, a host of old complaints and exaggerations, came pouring out. The U.S. Army had ruined her life, did he know that? They had trained her to be an ace and then consigned her to a life running back and forth between a turquoise washer and dryer. "I never really had any meaningful work," Frieda said.

"Almost nobody has meaningful work. You just shine the pants off your butt to stay above water." Hadn't he respected her flying all those years? There she'd been, flitting among the stars while he babysat the boys, smoking a lonely cigar, watching *Your Show of Shows,* a man ahead of his time, a feminist before anybody knew the word.

"Do you realize how much time we spend disagreeing?" Frieda asked. "Look at the Knoblocks. It could happen to us."

"But Knoblock is a jockstrap," Milt said. "I'm not like him."

"We're both like Knoblock. We're breathing down each other's necks. I spend my mornings with sick people. Some of them are dying, Milt, but at least they don't expect *me* to cure them."

Milt had removed all the pepperoni from his half of the pizza and stacked it into a cold, greasy pile, which he now offered to Frieda. She pushed it behind the napkin holder.

"I feel like I'm being turned into something I'm not. That's it!" he said, struck with insight. "I used to be treated like a man—with respect, a little fear even. Now people treat me like an old douche bag."

Frieda imagined him, for the first time in her life, as an old woman. The sexes did look more alike as they aged, as if turning into a parody of each other. She remembered her two years in the WASP when she had been treated—almost—like a man. Afterward, she was an outsider again, a woman living apart in a flannel-soft world that men inhabited only long enough to spread their genes around. That was the sociology of it. The rest of it was messier—love songs and bag ladies and young men dying in foreign wars or drug wars or gang wars. "I don't think I can help you with that one," she said.

Milt's eyes filled up again.

"But you can talk to me about it as much as you need to," Frieda added, then immediately regretted. Somewhere, in a book or on a talk show, she'd learned that if a person complained to you about a problem three times without doing anything about it, you became part of the problem, the way people who tolerated alcoholics actually enabled them to go on drinking.

———

Frieda snapped awake, her lap illuminated in the dark compartment by an overhead spot. She was on the bus home, her book open under the reading lamp, the moon dogging her in the window.

She looked at the page. Wasn't it miraculous how books waited for you?—the women in the harem all there, eyes inscrutable above their veils. Shame and charm, that's where she'd left off. According to the author, they may have derived from the same word.

She and Milt had talked about the photographs. The look on Milt's face when they fell out of Irv's jacket was not disapproval but surprise—surprise that Irv had a single idea left in his head. And it was a pretty good one, Frieda thought. Milt admitted he liked the pictures. They discussed buying their own Polaroid, maybe even a video camera. "Before everything shrivels up," Milt had said.

At her side, Milt snored fitfully, like an old bear in his den inhaling the first stirrings of spring. Soon he would awaken and lumber back into consciousness, into desire, full of the delicious hunger that came from surviving one more season.

Rapture

This happened to a woman in the off-season in the part of the world once called the Spanish Main. When the tourist trade is light there, the islanders sustain themselves with fishing, ship-building, and the manufacture of thatch rope, with shark skin and green turtles and a local breed of pony. The woman, Janet, had believed she was dying for more than a year. Her doctors said there was nothing seriously wrong; she was merely suffering from a panic disorder. But the attacks were riveting—a feverish, heart-pounding fanfare to her own mortality.

At 24,720 feet, the Cayman Trench, one of the deepest places on the Earth, resembles a cobalt channel through the aquamarine of the Caribbean. White lines border either side of it like lane markers on a highway, the result of water churning into frothy surf as it breaks across the craggy, coral-laden walls of the trench. Janet floated there, suspended in a vibrant blue-green light that seemed to have no source. Pale gold vertical shafts intersected the blue, like transparent swords plunging into the floor. In the gauzy silence, she heard her own breathing and an odd, regular pounding, as if someone far away were using a hydraulic drill.

She looked down at her pink and black dive-skin, borrowed for the occasion from her best friend. "Take mine," Rae had insisted. "Save yourself the expense." The pink was a delicate hue found only on the inside of certain human organs and flower petals. *The world is a colorful seduction.* She had once written that down. The hungry greens of the trees, always reaching, the billowing white clouds scudding by like the great wind-filled sails of the buccaneers who plundered the Main. And the ocean itself, the lapidary polish of its turquoise shallows.

A wiggly silver ball like a droplet of mercury from a broken thermometer passed in front of Janet. When she touched it, it wobbled apart into several smaller balls, like a cell dividing. Joy coursed through her body at this discovery. The silver balls ascended in a loose chain, like pearls spilling from a string. No, like a giggle made visible. She had always gotten the worst giggles in Bible History. Ancient Professor Schumaker, his mind permanently tethered to the stacks of plaster cuneiform tablets in his basement office, remained largely oblivious to the brisk traffic in notes passing furtively from desk to desk, the sotto voce jokes. The Hittites and Canaanites. The Lucites and Dendrites. The guffaws she suppressed were monumental, tuba-sized. Her stomach cramped with the effort of it while a luscious heat spread through her body ending in flushed cheeks and lips bitten bloodless. By the end of class, the trapped laughter threatened to steam from every pore and burst from her mouth and nose.

Tired, she kneeled against a hillock. It was soft and slimy as the lip of a pond. When she swam forward seconds later, she saw light pooling in faint tracks in the sand. She would follow them, wherever they led.

———

Janet and Gordon planned to stay friends. Besides, they had paid for the vacation months in advance and couldn't get a refund. It would be their last week as husband and wife.

The counseling had helped at first, cooling their heated arguments. Gordon was animated and talkative, but after a while, Janet could see that all they had accomplished was a facility in naming their differences, describing them in aching detail. The counselor congratulated them for not using blaming words, but inside, each still resented the other for the scarified wounds. Twenty-five years of marriage reduced to a polemic debate that both sides lost.

One morning at breakfast, Janet asked Gordon if he could spend five minutes a day talking to her. *Just five,* she had repeated. Gordon's eyes scanned the chevron wallpaper in the kitchen alcove, then he shook his head. "That's your definition of love, not mine."

Janet's whole face quivered. "I always assumed you were a dreamer, but you never had a dream of our life, did you? You just made it up as you went along." All of a sudden she felt clear-headed, almost serene.

"All I know is I've spent our entire marriage trying to second-guess you, to please you," he muttered. She had never seen Gordon cry, but now a few tears ran down his cheeks. "Instead of being pleased, you've lost respect for me." So each of them had come to some kernel, some version of the truth of their lives.

She pictured Gordon above her in the dive boat, his face shiny with sunscreen, his long-sleeved business shirt a white puff against the blue of the sky, like a sail snapping in the wind. Yes, just like a sail—full of movement and energy but without volition.

———

The depth changed abruptly. She drifted down and found herself on a ledge massed with brilliant sponges and corals. Above her, the light continued to flicker and dance. A school of large fish swam close, inspecting her, their bodies spangled silver discs. They nosed her tentatively, like dogs, then flashed back into the depths in a luminous zigzag.

A wall loomed at the edge of her vision, pocked and rough, as if it had been strafed. A bed of pink and orange anemones—fringed globes atop slender stems—waved at her from a shelf on the wall. They were pulsating, their centers opening and closing. Awe prickled through her as she touched the fringe. It felt like flesh. She remembered the drawings of fallopian tubes back in seventh grade at the girls-only assembly—staring at the screen where a filmstrip called "Growing Up, Girls to Women" unreeled her biological destiny. Apparently there was some kind of fruit stand inside her body—a pear-shaped uterus, the pituitary gland like a pistachio nut, ovaries resembling walnuts. Lobes buried deep in the cartoon girl's brain began to throb and glow, sending to the uterus, breasts, and ovaries streams of red arrows, like a military plan of attack. The fallopian tubes with their fringed openings waved the eggs in as they popped out of the ovary. She had not gotten her period yet, unlike most of the girls. In another three months, at the age of thirteen and a half, she would discover the tributary of blood in her pajama bottoms, proof of a distant if inner geography as mysterious as the source of the Nile.

The panic attacks sometimes lasted ten minutes, sometimes four hours. Her heart would pound and her lips would go numb and cool. Noises became muted and unintelligible, as if her ears were packed with cotton wool. She sweated and shook and her teeth chattered. It felt as if someone had a gun to her head. The doctors checked her heart, then referred her to a psychiatrist. Even when the medication—Xanax eased down to Klonopin—helped, she still believed she was going to die. Even after the pap smear came back negative, followed by the mammogram and ultrasound, EKG and chest X-ray, still she knew with complete certainty that she was dying.

They had jumped into waist-deep water from the dive boat, spreading outward in a circle, each with a buddy. *Oh, look at that stingray, that seahorse, that crab!* Earl was the name of her buddy, a polite and eager young Texan who was an experienced diver. "I'm going to stick close to her," he had assured Gordon. Due to a punctured eardrum in childhood, Gordon had never learned to swim. He lounged on the bow of the boat, a fishing reel set on drag in one hand, a copy of the London *Times* in the other. "I'm gonna stick to her like a wad of chewing gum." "Thanks very much," Gordon said. "It's her first real dive." Though Janet loved the water and had snorkeled for years, she'd been certified the day before at Cemetery Reef, where the depth was a scant twenty feet. It had taken just under two hours.

Where was Earl now? Janet vaguely wondered. She swam off to investigate a hole in the wall for eels.

Ten years earlier, she had begun buying art supplies without purpose, piling them untouched into a closet off the guest room. Then one day, when the closet was half-full, she sorted through her treasures—thick Arches paper, Windsor and Newton watercolors, an expensive set of French curves. The children were old enough to drive. Janet had time at last. She might actually save herself from the fate of all the women in her family, which was to spend their later years as visitors in other people's lives, doting on grandchildren, nieces and nephews, volunteering for charities.

She was very fortunate: she had a little money of her own, enough to live in a small apartment and pay the utility bill after the divorce. She hardly ever referred to herself as an artist or to her work as art. In the late nineties she completed *Openings,* using lipsticks, knitting needles, bead necklaces, tampons, wedding lace, half-eaten chocolate bars, recipe cards—the assorted debris of her life. The exhibit traveled through the South and was photographed for *Art Forum.* A woman in

Raleigh, North Carolina, wrote to Janet, interspersing praise for the show with sad episodes from her own history. But the work wasn't about money or career or fan mail. Her art pieces were simply the only unique objects in her life. They came from and belonged exclusively to her.

———

Tinged with gray, the colors paled. In place of the lush marine faubourgs with vibrant domes and steeples of orange, red, and pink, the coral formations were stone-colored. The water had darkened, though faint shimmers of light still penetrated the semigloom. She clicked on her underwater torch and the colors regained their bright allure. No other lights shone nearby, she noticed. That's when the idea crawled forward in her mind, blind as an earthworm seething up through leaf litter. *Alone.* Was she alone? Jagged and clear as a shard of glass, the idea began to merge with the watery surround. She tried to evaluate it—*a-lone*—the two syllables that should have alerted her to danger but instead dissolved into pure vocables that signified a mysterious and intense pleasure. In some fashion, she foggily concluded, the deepest joy would be hers and hers alone.

———

She had not realized how attractive she was until she had aged beyond her beauty. Gordon was handsome, too, with a ruddy complexion and luxuriant black hair, a thick curl of which grew from his widow's peak and hung like a rose over his broad forehead. Gordon was a good father when the children were small. He was in graduate school then, studying geology, a devoted house-husband. They often commented on how sunny life was with two young children in their bungalow in Coral Gables, and they didn't mean just the weather. They were grateful, not peevishly unaware of their blessings like so many couples. Just the sight of her children's faces made Janet joyful.

"Hormones," Rae concluded years later. "That happiness was mostly hormones, don't you think, looking back at it?" Rae had a penchant for the balder truths. Oh Rae, she was going to miss Rae. They had known each other since they were four years old. Rae had gone to law school when everyone became a career woman in the seventies. How ridiculous! Janet caught herself. She wouldn't miss Rae. Rae would miss *her.* It was difficult to imagine. Better to follow the brine shrimp skittering in the rocky crevices, the pellucid sea cucumber excreting its cloudy jet.

———

She had slept with only six men, including two brief affairs while she was married. If you added the awkwardness of the act together with the amount of time it took to feel at ease, it almost wasn't worth the trouble. All those movies and books in which women gasped and moaned, reaching their pleasure automatically: lies. She and Gordon used to call it the Charlton Heston version of sex, because it was more like bad acting than the truth. Oh, she had come, of course, with regularity, but it had never been easy. It had required finely tuned fingers, tongues, and battery-operated toys.

The water became more substantial, thickened into a navy-colored soup. What was that old TV show in which a splat of ink jumped out of an inkwell, shaping itself into a creature? She was like that creature now, swimming about in the inkwell, her way lit by flashlight. The wall was smoother, bedecked with fewer living things. Even with her flashlight, she could not see the bottom or top of it.

She regarded her flipper-clad feet dangling below her. The water felt delicious, rushing in runnels through her hair and around her wrists and neck. Craving more bare skin to enjoy the sensation, she bent double and removed her flippers; they dropped away into the blue chasm beneath her. The water swarmed between her toes as she splayed them; it felt cushiony, as if she had plunged her foot into a thick bed of moss. Slippery as birth, which verged on ecstasy: first the pain, then the small faces, the tiny fingers and tinier fingernails, the essence of all that was human in six pounds of flesh. How different the two infants had looked, their small reddened faces screwed up in the cavernous glare of the delivery room, their bodies still coated with vernix, the white wax of the womb. Then the nurses washed them off and they cried, mewling and voracious. A sound only another human could recognize as the beginnings of love and need. Now they would be fine without her.

She descended ever so slowly, the pearl in the Prell shampoo bottle. The space around her narrowed, like the neck of a funnel. She felt myriad currents on her body, cool licks, then warmer ones, then cool again. The blue deepened to bootblack except for the area lit by her flashlight, which began to dim.

———

The divers searched until nightfall, sectioning the sea with buoy markers. The coast guard dispatched a cutter and two open launches. A Panamanian fishing vessel and two shrimp trawlers pitched in, stretching the dragnet across the blank blue surface.

With Gordon, the dive operator reviewed Janet's certification application from the day before. "She was taking something for pain, it says here." He pointed to Janet's scrawl. "Celebrex."

"For her arthritis," Gordon said. "But I know she didn't take it yesterday or today."

"Good. But was she taking anything else?"

Gordon gazed at Janet's handwriting, touching it with his forefinger. *Age: 52. Sex: Female.* Under next of kin she had listed their daughter as well as Gordon. *Medications: Synthroid, Celebrex.* The Klonopin. She hadn't listed it but he was sure she had taken it. He remembered the tangerine tablet held up like a tiny sun between her fingers before she popped it in her mouth.

The dive operator explained that the Klonopin would have concentrated in her blood in proportion to the depth. At forty feet, it would have been three times stronger, producing euphoria and disorientation and a blessed insentience to pain.

Later, people said the certification wasn't adequate, that the dive operator should have questioned her more extensively about medications, explaining the deadly effects of compression. Americans took so many pills.

———

A day and a night must have passed before she reached the floor of the trench, which through unmanned exploration had been determined to be as flat as a roadbed. The temperature would have dropped with the depth, hovering just above freezing when she reached the plateau at 4,000 feet. She would have grown colder and then numb, her mind still sorting through memories that shifted like the bits of colored glass in a kaleidoscope, her time on earth displayed as a series of elaborate symmetries. The tube would have kept turning, the tiny shards clicking into place against the angled mirror, transforming the jumble of her life into patterns as rapturous as the rose windows in a cathedral.

The Hottest Spot on Earth

She always had handouts: that's how you could tell that Dr. Patricia Warde was a college professor and not some Vegas bimbo. What a show-off, Jill thought, snatching a packet from the surf of paper floating above the rows of pink upholstered chairs. The top page, the cover of a recent Slash novel, caught Jill's eye. In a pen-and-ink drawing, Captain Kirk and Commander Spock sprawled nude on the bridge of the *Enterprise*, Spock's member (always drawn with two ridges like planetary rings) nestled in Kirk's hand. She stuffed the packet into her tote and picked her way through the crowd toward Patricia at the front of the room. It was the second day of the annual Slash Writers' Convention and the two women were scheduled to appear on a panel together.

Patricia was fiddling with a comb dangling from her coif. The woman labeled herself a feminist scholar, but everything about her—long, curly blond hair, miniskirt, big noisy earrings—proclaimed *I like sex* and *I like men*. Jill thought of feminists as humorless women who didn't shave and wore army camo. She had said as much to Patricia the day before. Patricia had replied that whether Jill knew it or not, she was a "proto-feminist." Proto as in protoplasm? As in an unthinking blob of goo?

Jill felt patronized by Patricia. She suspected that Patricia entertained ideas about her that she couldn't understand. Ultimately it didn't matter. Jill was a pornographer; she wasn't trying to learn anything from the professor. On the contrary, Patricia was the one who had been studying Jill along with the other Slash writers at their last three annual meetings. *Instruments,* she called her questionnaires and surveys, as if little surgical tools were squirreled inside the booklets. The Slashers happily participated, convinced that Patricia's probing conferred stature on their work. In return for their cooperation, Patricia was a regular keynoter and gave hilarious lectures on popular culture. She was always comparing Slash to Shakespeare, claiming the Bard hadn't intended to write masterpieces, merely the bawdy entertainment of his times. *Except in retrospect, Shakespeare is not high art,* she had pronounced. Fatuous bull, Jill thought. The Slashers had applauded, happy to be a part of world literature.

Jill had always suspected that Patricia had a hidden agenda. She took out a subscription to *Film Femina,* the journal Patricia edited. But it was full of terminology too obscure for the dictionary, such as *structural antithesis* and *deconstructive fallacy,* and shed no light on the situation. Still, even without a clear idea of what Patricia thought of her and the other Slashers, Jill knew that Patricia was more than a professor coolly observing her subjects. She would not have been surprised to learn that Dr. Warde regarded the Slash writers as her troop of chimps and herself as Jane Goodall.

Patricia Warde admired Jill Simons, the queen of Slash, one of its earliest practitioners. Jill had produced eleven Slash novels, nine based on *Star Trek* and two Mel Gibson/Danny Glover spin-offs—*Lethal Romance* and *Lovely Weapon*. But instead of sisterhood, there was between the two women what Patricia envisioned as a patriarchal fence consisting of fashion and diets and recipes for gourmet meals in less than thirty minutes—consisting, in essence, of men, whom Patricia loved with all their hairiness and pent-up emotionality. It was the fence that had divided women from time immemorial, so that their discourse was reduced to hurried endearments over white pickets while their husbands' underwear consorted with the breeze.

Patricia watched as Jill made her way to the front of the room. Jill wore an emerald green satin blouse behind which her breasts jiggled. Framed by short, spiked brown hair, her throat and heavily made-up face flared like a torch. An orange stripe of peroxided hair not present the day before arced from ear to ear. What a metaphor, Patricia thought: a headband of rage! Surrounded by her protégés, Jill was the epitome of self-confidence. Patricia was confident, too, though she sometimes second-guessed herself. She had sorted out most of her life except whether she was happy. Since she wasn't actively unhappy, she considered herself happy by default.

Patricia observed Jill stopping to chat with friends in the audience, her fingers dancing with light from many diamond rings. Probably Diamoniques, thought Patricia. *Shut her up forever with a diamond.* Her version of the ad slogan. She and Daniel had exchanged simple gold bands. Patricia wondered what Jill's husband did for a living, but it went against her principles to ask. Daniel was a musicologist. Patricia wore earplugs at home, even in bed, to scale the wall of constant noise—Daniel humming as he read, Daniel listening to a CD or the TV. The next thing she knew, his hand would be between her legs, the covers would be billowing from the bed like a wave silently crashing—

"We're almost ready to start," Jill said, pulling up her chair.

She never misses a chance to take charge, thought Patricia.

The audience had grown silent, their heads bent studiously over the packets of dirty drawings.

The topic of the three-woman panel discussion was "Cashing in on Slash Imagery." Stacks of fanzines formed a parapet at one end of the speakers' table. Jill sat sandwiched between Patricia and Zen Frank, a short, red-faced woman in her late thirties, the author of a successful Trek novel called *Where No Woman Has Gone Before.*

Jill muffled her microphone with her hand. "Even more men than yesterday," she whispered to Patricia.

Jill considered Slash a female occupation. Few men could manage it. They seemed to forget that they were writing pornography for women—not for men, not for men and women, but for women only—and they'd abandon the Slash formula: two powerful straight men (they were never depicted as gay) fell in love, temporarily. And Slash was never violent, despite the name, which referred only to the way the books were listed for sale in the fanzines. "K/S" meant Kirk and Spock fell in love. "Sop—T/F" indicated Tony Soprano and his enforcer, Fiorio, got together. "I count seven guys today," Jill said.

"They worry me," said Patricia. "Remember when men first took up quilts?"

"Men are making quilts?"

"You didn't know?"

"I'm not really into quilts—"

"They don't actually sew them," Patricia explained. "They let the women of China do that. They just design them. They're also designing rugs for the women of Turkey to weave." Patricia often launched herself into diatribes. "It's all the same thing. Why do you think *The Bridges of Madison County* was so popular?"

"I beg your pardon?" Was Patricia *trying* to make her feel stupid or was she the master of the non sequitur? Either way, she had the charm of a computer virus.

"I'm sorry, I didn't mean to quiz you." Patricia's hand grazed Jill's shoulder, like a bird not quite landing. "It's just so typical. Women cook, men are chefs. Women write hundreds of romances a year, but let a man write one and voilà, he's not a hack, he's an auteur."

"Yeah," Jill said, the best she could muster. She picked up the gavel and rapped it on the podium.

Zen Frank began with what Jill considered the miracle and mystery of Slash, the reason she wrote it and read it. "Reading about men falling helplessly in love with each other the way women fall in love with men turns women on." Zen paused for a moment, letting the words settle. "In my novel the men love each other the way women love their *children,* except it's eroticized."

The audience buzzed.

"The maternal imagery was serendipitous," she confided. "I'd just had my first child. Let's look at page two of the handout." She read aloud:

> "Spock peeled off the clothes frozen to Kirk's body after a half hour on the planet's surface. Kirk looked so vulnerable, like a baby about to be diapered. He touched Kirk's hairless chest—a big beautiful baby—and imagined himself rubbing baby oil on him."

"I'm sprinkling a lot of lactation in my next novel. I've got a male science officer who drinks an estrogen cocktail so he can breast-feed a dying crewman. It's steamy."

Jill was knocked out by this innovation. She could instantly imagine characters abusing it, too, in group nursing parties. A good thing taken to excess could spice up the plot.

Next, Patricia presented a carefully reasoned argument likening the values of the old *Star Trek* to the liberalism of JFK's New Frontier. "The old *Star Trek* was hopeful, optimistic, idealistic. That's why people are still writing and reading a thousand Trek spin-off books a year."

Baloney, Jill thought. The only leftist thing about the old *Star Trek* was that the male characters wore it on the left, every one of them. Trekkies claimed that Dr. McCoy's was actually a zucchini.

Jill had given many of the writers in the room their start and was a popular speaker. She liked going last, as if she were the featured band and the others warm-up acts. Her own career had begun when she sent a few scripts to the *Star Trek: The Next Generation* people. They had all come back paper-clipped to brief printed notes explaining they weren't right for the show. Jill suspected they had never been read. After that, she began writing to please herself, discovered Slash, and put her heart and soul into it.

She spoke of identity and equality, of love between powerful male equals, which was the Slash formula.

"Unlike porno for men, in Slash you can't have sex without love, and love is the result of bonding."

She gave a few examples from her novels.

"We women bond easily, like squares of flannel that stick together. But men are more competitive. For them to bond and fall in love, there must be danger and isolation—a star about to go nova, a short air supply, Mel Gibson lashed to a Catherine wheel."

"Not anymore!" Patricia interrupted. She removed a DVD from her briefcase and held it aloft. "May I?"

Jill nodded.

Patricia flipped up the screen of her laptop on the table in front of her and inserted the disk. "Let me show you the latest development in Slash. No dire emergencies required. This is called a 'song tape.'"

The reedy voice of Marlon Brando singing "I'll Know When My Love Comes Along" faded in as baseball players trotted onto a field. With clever editing, someone had produced a three-minute Slash version of a Cincinnati Reds game. The pitcher ran his tongue over his lips as the camera cut to the catcher's crotch. Longing glances from the dugout, the eyes and mouths in extreme close-up, were intercut with a collage of fetching butt-shots. "Slash baseball," Patricia said. "It opens up a whole new way of looking at sports for women."

Jill envied Patricia for receiving the DVD. She must remember to ask her who had sent it. She could make her own song tapes. She already had a CD burner and a terrific mailing list. She'd just need to buy editing software.

By the time the Slashers finished watching the DVD for the third time, the panel session was over.

That evening after dinner, Patricia waited in a small crowd for the elevator in the food court. Like everything in Las Vegas, the elevator doors were extravagant—polished brass with a female nude etched across the seam between them. Done in the Art Deco style, the figure was abstracted into two svelte, reciprocating curves of breasts and buttocks. *Like parentheses,* she immediately realized. *Woman depicted as merely parenthetical, an aside in the cultural conversation.* She jotted her thoughts and a sketch in a small leather notebook.

The elevators were slow. Day and night people were gambling, eating, going to shows, and attending conventions. Neon had replaced sunlight in the circadian cycle. Finally the car arrived and the brass woman split in half, taking all the passengers into her hollow body.

In her hotel room, Patricia read the last thirty pages of *Ro-*

mantic Enterprise, Jill's new novel, and smoothed the cover flat. It took a moment to readjust to her surroundings, as if she were returning from a trip. She regarded the pastel haze of downtown Las Vegas. A pyramid-shaped hotel prodded the sky. Beyond it, the suburbs twinkled in a grid, like a busy switchboard. Patricia had read all of Jill's novels. The woman was a natural, a brilliant savage hacking her way through life with the machete of her mind. What a clanky metaphor—not like Jill's, which were unobtrusive and clever. Jill, she guessed, was free of doubt and burning ambition, and therefore didn't need the armor of irony to confront the world. Patricia imagined her shopping at The Limited, trying on clothes while the tremulous voices of chanteuses wafted through the cubicles. Pseudo-French would be just the ticket for Jill.

Patricia had tried repeatedly to embrace popular culture, but instead she turned it over with tongs, she sectioned it, and slid it on glass under a microscope. Except for film. Patricia loved film. There was only one downside: she could not conceptualize her life as anything but a series of rapid plot switches, her existence reduced to a collage of familiar melodramas. She believed everyone in the country born after 1950 was doomed to watch their lives from the outside, as characters gliding along well-worn plot paths. At the moment, she felt as if she had been cast in a film about two women who were destined to become friends even though they disliked each other. Patricia was certain that she and Jill shared deep affinities and that Jill also sensed the two of them moving through the hackneyed friendship arc. But Jill was feistier and more creative; she might resist the pull of the narrative. They

were like those old Scottie dog magnets: back to back, they re-
pelled each other. But if one turned slightly, they would click
together. The same force that kept them apart would unite
them. That was the plot of this movie.

———

The temperature would reach the mid-nineties by afternoon,
so on Saturday morning Patricia had loaded her backpack
with protein bars, sunscreen, bottled water, and in case of a
real emergency, a chocolate bar with a couple of ice cubes in a
Ziploc bag.

August sunshine silvered the tour bus as it pulled onto the
highway. She watched as Las Vegas, flat and white as a plate,
quickly receded from view in the rear windows. Las Vegas
was a blatantly commercial city where the sex lives of aliens
had never raised an eyebrow. The Slashers had always met
there and always offered the option of a group trip to a local
attraction. They had already toured the Grand Canyon and
Hoover Dam. This year's destination was the Nevada Nuclear
Test Site, now maintained like a park by the Department of
Energy, which offered free bus charters. Located sixty-five
miles northwest of town in the desert, it was universally regarded as the mother of all sci-fi filmscapes.

The bus had picked them up at the hotel at nine A.M. Patricia had taken the aisle seat across from Jill. She had decided
to invite Jill to speak at a *Film Femina* meeting in the spring.
Knowing how easily she rubbed Jill the wrong way, she now
pondered the timing and terms of the invitation, her mind
leaping ahead to the reflected glory that would be hers when

Jill shed light on Slash, a catacomb of underground literature unknown in the mustier corridors of academe.

She watched the terrain slip by, a monotonous stretch of coarse sand swatched here and there with large rocks and the green of cacti and yuccas. No wildlife was evident, but the memory of a National Geographic special supplied her with snakes in burrows, lizards, and rats panting in slivers of shade.

The tour guide, wearing a gray government uniform like a postal worker's, plucked a microphone from the cubby above the dashboard and welcomed them aboard. She reviewed the history and geology of the site. There had been no above-ground testing for decades, though the range was still operational. More than six hundred bombs had been exploded, most of them underground. "Radioactively speaking," the guide said, "this is the hottest spot on Earth."

Patricia was shocked. Beyond the desert, in the cattle and sheep country, were there children hybridized with ruminants? With houseflies?

"I'm going to distribute your badges and paperwork now," the guide announced. "This is your identification tag while you're with us at the range. It also measures radiation exposure."

A murmur of concern passed through the rows of passengers.

"Routine," the guide assured them.

Would it turn blue or purple at the end of the trip, like a pregnancy test? Over the years, Patricia had waited in vain for dozens of acrylic columns and windows to indicate that motherhood was in her future.

"So it's still radioactive here?" a woman asked. The guide shook her head. "What if you're pregnant?" another called out.

"It's safe," the guide said. "The badge is just a formality."

———

The bus parked in the shadeless lot of the Visitors' Center, a low concrete building that resembled a bomb shelter, where they would be educated about the test sites before viewing them.

"Look." Jill pointed. "Drink machines. And candy machines. Can I get you a Coke, Patricia?" I will be friendly, she thought. I am a professional and this is business.

Patricia jumped at the show of warmth. "I'd love a Coke." She tightened the cap of her water bottle and stuffed it in her pack.

"You brought supplies?"

"I didn't think we'd get any food."

"Raisinets, Gummy Bears, Red Hots. Just like going to the movies," Jill crowed. She bought a box of Milk Duds.

The two women lingered over the Center's footage of underground tests. Jill was astonished by the palsied quaking of the desert, the concentric circles at ground zero glowing red and yellow beneath the surface. She would use it in a story or novel somewhere—the earth incandescent, rumbling as if it were about to pop its cork. "I didn't know about this underground stuff," she told Patricia. "I always pictured mushroom clouds. This is scarier."

"I guess the general public is ignorant of it." Patricia dabbed at her forehead with a handkerchief.

So now I'm the lowly general public, Jill thought. Dr. Warde was a clod, pure and simple. Jill fought the impulse to craft a nasty reply, and moved to the next exhibit.

Patricia, unaware of her gaffe, caught up with Jill. "I didn't know you could visit this place. I didn't even know it was here, so close to Las Vegas."

Ah, Jill thought, at last, a tad of humility.

The guide was calling on her bullhorn for them to board the bus. The rest of the visit would be conducted from inside the vehicle with the windows closed.

A landscape of weird monuments to war, the test site had been undisturbed since the late fifties. The bus crept past a mock-up town with puddled bridges and roofs, buildings blasted apart from the center like handfuls of pick-up sticks. Rebar lay everywhere, the bent licorice twists of giants. The guide said that there had been livestock in the early tests, goats and sheep. "Vaporized," she added without expression. Patricia remembered photos of Hiroshima's citizens reduced to sooty shadows on pavements and walls.

"This reminds me of Simba Safari," Jill said. "We drove through the whole park and never saw a lion. Creepy. Like this. No living things."

Patricia clucked in assent. Behind them, she noticed a second clutch of tourists bouncing along in an identical government bus. A guide stood braced at the front, speaking into a microphone. "Do you have children?" Patricia abruptly asked Jill.

"A thirteen-year-old, Suraya."

"That's a beautiful name."

"Everyone says so, but I wonder if I did her a favor, picking such an unusual name."

Zen Frank, who had been listening, swatted the idea away with her hand. "Kids have incredible names these days. Like Chastity and Planet, and that acting family, you know, River and Summer and Storm Phoenix. Unusual names are in."

"It's good," Patricia said. "People will remember her."

"No, she hates standing out. She's got her friends calling her 'Stump.'" Jill shook her head. "She's entered a rebellious phase. I should have stuck to an ordinary name, like Jane, or Susan."

"Don't blame yourself," Patricia said. "Adolescence is difficult no matter what your name is."

Jill reached across the aisle and briefly squeezed Patricia's hand.

The two tour buses pulled alongside the imposing chain-link gates where the journey had begun. "You've got twenty minutes to take pictures or use the bathroom." The guide gestured toward his and hers cement block restrooms. "But first I'm going to collect your IDs."

The passengers exited the vehicles and filed past, surrendering their badges.

"Do you measure them with a Geiger counter?" Jill asked. She was a stickler for details, details made a book.

"I'm not sure," the guide said.

"But they do it now, right?" Zen's voice was strained.

"No, I'm sorry if I gave that impression. We send them to a lab. They contact you if you've experienced an exposure."

"But, I'm nursing my baby," Zen said. "I need to know now."

The guide was unfazed. "On my tours, no one has ever turned in a hot badge."

"It must not be dangerous," Patricia reassured Zen, "or they wouldn't let people in to begin with."

"You trust the government?" A stranger from the other bus suddenly faced off with Patricia. The tall, wiry man repeated his question to the crowd, then, pointing to the guide, asked, "This *lackey*?"

Patricia was dumbfounded. His words hung in the air like a gunshot. The guide looked lost. Her cohort from the second tour bus hurried over and escorted her away from the throng.

"Richard!" someone shouted at the provocateur, loud enough for all to hear. The man looked toward the voice. "The guides are not decision makers. They can do nothing to change policy." An older woman made her way toward the man. "It's counterproductive to vent your anger on them."

He scuffed his feet on the rough pavement. "What about change that starts from below? If I could convert the guide she might say something to her boss, and then—"

"She'd get fired," the older woman said calmly. "The best you could hope for if you did change her mind is that she could afford to quit."

"I think we've stumbled into a graduate seminar," Patricia told Jill and Zen.

Richard sighed. "You're right. I'm still full of anger."

"And I have a lot of compassion for your anger." The mother figure patted the man's shoulder.

"And I," Patricia interjected in her most authoritative classroom voice, "have a couple of questions. Who are you people? Why are you hassling our guide?"

The older woman stepped forward, extending her hand. She was silver-haired, wearing a khaki skirt and checked blouse. A damp pink scarf drooped at her neck. "We're the Desert Consortium. We oppose nuclear testing."

"And a lot of other wrongdoing," Richard added. "Child labor, oppression of migrant workers, corporate-controlled media—"

The woman cut him off. "My name is Roberta Blierstein. Some of our members, like Richard here, are full-time activists."

Richard and Patricia introduced themselves to each other.

"I'll be damned," Jill said, from the edge of the conversation, "I had no idea." She shook hands with the two protesters.

"It started with the testing, but then we formed the consortium," Richard explained, "because we agreed on so many issues. We were all against the war in Iraq and NAFTA. We oppose food irradiation and water fluoridation, pesticide spraying for West Nile virus."

"And we're all pro-choice," Roberta said. She had a cheerful face, no makeup, apple cheeks.

"Fascinating," Patricia said. "So you are always organized and ready to stage a protest?"

"Correct," said Roberta.

Jill's mind was spinning. There could be a planet, Do-minia, similar to the planet in the old *Star Trek* that waged virtual computer wars instead of actual battles, but then murdered its flesh-and-blood citizens. Life was perfect on Dominia, but because people still had a hunger for dissent, two violent factions were always battling for reform. *Hunger for Dissent!* with a cover of Spock and Kirk nude-wrestling over their principles, having been recruited by . . . Yes! Something in the water or air determined your allegiance. No, microchips implanted at birth. Everything was arbitrary and rational and pointless.

"And what does your group do?" Roberta asked.

Zen Frank answered. "We're all writers."

"Published writers?" Richard's face brightened.

"I've only published one novel," Zen said, "but my friend Jill, here, has eleven."

Richard whistled through his teeth. "Whew. Great. Books are a great platform."

"We just try to entertain our readers," Jill said. "We don't have any axes to grind."

"Oh," said Richard.

"Richard once nearly mashed a cream pie in Daddy Bush's face," Roberta said. "It was on the national news."

The bullhorns crackled on, announcing that the buses would depart in ten minutes. The engines turned over. There was a short line for the toilet, and Jill joined it. Behind the guardhouse she noticed a metallic brown vehicle, a cross between a Brinks van and a mail truck. She couldn't decipher the initials on it. Two men wearing green shirts and trousers leaned against it, talking.

When Jill rejoined them, Roberta, Richard, Patricia, and Zen had wandered back through the gates into the testing range, and Roberta was pointing out a desert orchid. The flower was lovely, with narrow, curved petals like talons, and an amber center freckled with darker brown. Jill longed to touch it, but stared reverently instead.

She glanced back toward the parking lot: the buses had pulled onto the road! She was incredulous. Had the guides never heard of counting? Were they blind, mean, stupid, or all three? And what about the Slashers? Hadn't they noticed three people were missing?

The men in green jumped from the brown vehicle. Before Jill knew what was happening she heard a loud click as her hands were locked together in orange plastic handcuffs. Speechless, she watched Roberta and Richard roll up their shirtsleeves and extend their wrists politely—as if they were about to get a manicure. No, like two dogs trained to sit up and beg together. And their goddamn puppy paws were wrapped with a white binding of some sort. As Jill's wrists began to chafe inside her cuffs, it dawned on her that the tape was a protective layer and that they must have known they were going to be arrested.

"Nice to see you again, Officer," Roberta said, ever the group leader. "But I'm afraid there's been a mix-up."

"What might that be, ma'am?" the officer asked.

"These three women are not part of the protest. They just missed their bus."

"That's a whole lotta too bad," the officer said. He herded them toward the brown vehicle, which, Jill realized now, was a glitzy paddy wagon.

"I'm so sorry," Roberta said. "We always forewarn the police when we're going to stage a protest. Otherwise there's nobody here to arrest us."

"And the protest is what exactly?" Jill asked. The five of them reached the van.

"Trespassing on government property. We just step over the line after the tour ends," Roberta said. "I wish I had thought to mention it to the three of you. I'm so sorry."

"We got busy talking," Richard added. "I'm sorry, too."

They climbed into the vehicle.

Jill gasped. "My tote bag! I dropped it. Could you get it for me, please, Officer? My whole life's in there."

"No problem." The officer trudged across the parking lot and returned promptly with the bag swinging from his shoulder. As he handed it over to Jill in the paddy wagon, it flipped upside down and everything tumbled out. Kirk and Spock landed on top. The officer lifted the packet and paged through it, his eyes widening.

"That's nothing, some scholarly research materials," Patricia jumped in. "It's mine. I have more in here. Two, three . . . maybe six copies." She pointed toward her backpack. "She got hers from me."

The officer retrieved the backpack and dug past the food,

candy, and water to the packets. After a moment, he announced he was confiscating them. He scribbled a receipt for Patricia, then dropped Jill's packet and the backpack onto the floor of the paddy wagon. "I've seen worse, but these still might be obscene." A smile died on his face as he tucked the drawings into his back pocket and slammed shut the van doors.

Richard cocked his head as he paged through the upside-down booklet with his foot. "We're opposed to censorship, too," he announced.

———

Through two narrow windows in the van Jill watched the sky darken, threatening rain. Patricia had begun lecturing Roberta and Richard on Slash. The paddy wagon rumbled toward Las Vegas.

"I get it now, I can see it," Richard said thoughtfully. "It validates female love."

Patricia gave him a double thumbs-up from her handcuffs.

"I really don't see how they could charge obscenity," Roberta said. "They're just pen-and-ink sketches. You should see the posters for the peep shows downtown."

"I feel anxious," Zen whispered to Jill. "I'm worried about my baby, back at the hotel with my husband. He needs me." She bit her lip and her eyes grew large with tears.

"He'll be all right, he won't even notice you're gone." Jill pulled Zen toward her and tried to blot out the ever-instructive Dr. Warde, who was talking a mile a minute.

———

Jail: the cauldron, the crucible. In her article "Justice in a Box," Patricia had discussed the semiotics of jail scenes: westerns with grizzled miners picking their teeth; young Americans rotting in the backwaters of Turkey and Pakistan; Susan Hayward paraded to her execution in *I Want to Live*. But jail also held the potential for triteness, for schmaltz. If she ever wrote about her time in jail, she would downplay the drama, keep things light. Dying is easy, comedy is hard. Who said that?

Zen had phoned her husband and he was on his way across town with the baby. Even though it was long distance, the sheriff had allowed Jill and Patricia to call home. At two o'clock on a Saturday afternoon, both husbands were out; the women left messages on machines. The Desert Five (Patricia's coinage) would go before the judge at six. If they were lucky, they'd be back at the hotel in plenty of time for the Slash banquet.

The four women shared a cell. Zen decided to meditate. She sat ZaZen on the concrete floor and neither spoke nor answered when spoken to. Perched on the top bunk of the only bed, Roberta pored over a day-old newspaper. Richard had finally exhausted his anger; they could hear him snoring in a cell down the hall.

Roberta and Richard would plead guilty with an explanation: civil disobedience. They'd be released without bail, Roberta said, the routine procedure for nonviolent protest.

Patricia and Jill slumped next to each other on the bottom

bunk, strategizing. They would explain to the judge that they never intended to trespass.

"Let's say we were distracted by the orchid and missed the bus," Patricia proposed. Jill agreed. If charged with obscenity, they would accept a public defender.

They sat in silence for a few moments. Then Jill decided to spill the beans. "I've read your magazine, *Film Femina*," she said, "but it's like reading Klingon."

"Scholarly journals are like that. I guess the average person wouldn't be up to it."

"I guess you have no manners," Jill snapped.

Patricia flushed a pale shade of red. "I only meant that occasionally my PhD is good for something. It's pretty irrelevant day to day."

Jill wasn't appeased. "It's just useless gobbledygook if you ask me," she retaliated. "I think scholars are parasites."

Patricia winced.

Jill relented. "What I'm trying to say is that maybe you should write for the lay reader, like for *Parade* magazine. You could be the Stephen Hawking of Slash fiction."

"Do you really think the average person would be interested?"

"Stop saying 'average person,' okay? There is no such thing. Anyway, people don't know what they are interested in until they find it." Jill was thinking of herself. In the Jacksonville Library she browsed the shelves to ignite her imagination. She had modeled an entire civilization, the Trantrit, located in the eye of the Horsehead Nebula, on the extinct Calusa Indians of southwest Florida. She liked to feed her head. "People enjoy seeing through the bullshit. They want the truth. They notice things, like that Captain Kirk was always on the make. That most of the black actors, like Worf, wear so much makeup they really do look alien. They want someone to tell them why, expose the hypocrisy." Her eyes narrowed with intensity. "Did you know there were only two episodes where Kirk didn't kiss somebody? He was exploring the universe, all right—with his tongue."

"Very astute." Patricia turned toward Jill, her eyes shining with admiration. "You're a natural scholar."

"I hope that's better than being an average scholar."

Patricia smiled. "I wish you lived closer. You could take a course. We could be friends." She blushed at her own directness.

Light flickered in the orange zone of Jill's hair. "I'd have to take one of your courses to be your friend?" She waited. Patricia rummaged in her pocket for a tissue. She blew her nose.

"We aren't that different, you know, or we wouldn't both be in this jail cell." Jill was fuming. "You aren't as important and special as you think."

"But I don't think I'm special or important. Most of the time, I think I'm completely unimportant. I am always justifying my existence to myself, for your information." Patricia hated herself now. The movie of the two of them had jumped the projector. She could not imagine even one celluloid frame of the next scene.

At six-ten they were ushered into the courtroom, a pleasant chamber with oiled wood paneling. Judge Elaine Creedy was a middle-aged woman with platinum blond hair and creamy skin. She recognized Roberta and Richard, this being their fourth arrest. She ordered their release and asked them to please protest elsewhere.

As for Zen, Jill, and Patricia, once the judge learned they were not members of the Desert Consortium, she chastised them for inattention and dismissed the charge so that she could attend to the six potential counts of obscenity.

"Your Honor," Roberta jumped up from her seat. "If you charge them with obscenity, you have to charge me, too."

"Don't do this," the judge pleaded. "It's obvious that these people accidentally trespassed and that you accidentally came in possession of their print material."

Roberta glanced at Richard. "We could file an amicus brief."

"Mrs. Blierstein," said the judge. "There is no case yet. Your enthusiasm is premature."

Roberta sat down. Zen's husband had arrived with their baby, and the three of them huddled in a back row where Zen nursed the infant, partially shielded by her husband's Hawaiian shirt.

The officer described how the booklets came into his possession. He handed one to the judge. She riffled the pages, pausing here and there. "Las Vegas does not need another sleazy industry," she warned. "Where was this printed?"

"I made the photocopy you are holding in Pennsylvania, Your Honor." Patricia enjoyed saying "Your Honor" to a woman. She enjoyed being in a courtroom drama. Though she hadn't completely recovered from her confrontation with Jill, she was herself again, at least her classroom self.

"And to what purpose?"

Jill claimed they were book covers, their purpose to illustrate and entertain. Patricia claimed they were scholarly research materials. "Cultural artifacts, actually," she added.

The judge peered over her eyeglasses. "Which is it, fun or work?"

Taking turns, they explained themselves in more detail. What a team we could be, Patricia thought. Somehow she had insulted Jill. Hopefully Jill would figure out how harmless she was, how unintentional the insult had been.

"All right," the judge pondered aloud, "I'm going to take this under advisement, confer with the district attorney. You're all free to leave. Just make sure the bailiff knows how to reach you."

Carrying her baby in a sling, Zen waved good-bye and fled the courtroom, her husband following with diaper bag and stroller.

Outside the City Center, the Desert Five exchanged email addresses and wished one another well. Patricia and Jill took a taxi back to their hotel. It was still early; they wouldn't miss the evening festivities.

At the hotel, Jill and Patricia encountered Zen Frank and her family waiting in line for the cashier at the front desk. They inched forward in a clump of their luggage, three travelers taking refuge in a soft-sided fort. Jill and Patricia admired the baby, whose name was Bud. Zen confided that when she was meditating at the jail, each time she had allowed a thought about her baby to intrude, her breasts had leaked. "I am going to listen to my breasts," she told Jill and Patricia. "I'm going home right now." She hugged the two women and promised to stay in touch.

Jill raced to her room, stripped, showered, and turned on her laptop. An excellent typist, she proceeded to record everything she'd seen and felt that day and the sci-fi ideas that had arisen—the badges, the planet with the hunger for dissent, etc. Then she lay on the bed in her terry robe and allowed the day to wash over her. Patricia. A bit spoiled, extremely awkward. That speech in the paddy wagon, taking the blame for all the Slash drawings: noble. *It is a far, far better thing I do* noble. Pretty feet, though. In the jail, Patricia had removed her sneakers and Jill had noticed her milky feet with polished toenails like little bunches of fruit. And Zen. Novice author, novice mother. With a bland husband, but good-bland. All in all, a practical, rational woman. Practicing Buddhist. Oh boy, Jill realized with a jolt. The baby's name is short for Buddha!

━━

Patricia primped at the vanity in her room, relishing the thought of recounting her adventure to friends and colleagues. She might even include it in her *Film Femina* column: "Crossed Wires: Protest and Pornography." Could she draw any deeper insights from the coincidence? How about "Who

Protests for Pornography?" Did anyone? She hadn't a clue. But the day had energized her, whatever its outcome in print.

The narrative arc with Jill had fizzled (the picture of a rocket smoking back to Earth came to mind). But at least now they'd have something to talk about besides Slash. It might even turn into a private joke. Daniel's family had such a tradition. It took the form of a shot put, which appeared and disappeared among the possessions of the far-flung family members. Once, Daniel had discovered it inside his sleeping bag while traveling in the Andes. Someone had mailed it to his mother at a bed-and-breakfast in Boston. It routinely showed up, usually in a suitcase, at weddings and even at funerals, where it served as a reminder that the family endured, despite the death of one of its members. Patricia had never seen the much-mythologized object, though, as Daniel said, there wasn't much to see. No one in the family spoke of the shot put or its comings and goings. That was its supreme virtue: wordlessness, especially for Patricia, who often screwed things up by talking. What could she plant in Jill's suitcase or briefcase that would become their special object? It must have significance, be related somehow to this sojourn in Las Vegas. A casino chip? Too small, likely to get lost. It had to have heft and bulk, no moving parts so there was nothing to break. It had to be indestructible, like gold. Or iron.

Jill lectured the following year at the *Film Femina* meeting. The year after that, the two women wrote a magazine article together: "The Unibrow and the Unicorn: Ideas of Self-transformation on *Queer Eye for the Straight Guy*." They discussed cowriting a Slash novel, but it never happened.

Unbeknown to Patricia, Jill used her as the model for a computer gone benignly haywire, which assigned people to the wrong kinship groups on the planet Dramuma.

In the peripatetic screenplay Patricia composed in her head, wherever Jill traveled, an iron bar appeared in her luggage. She never grasped its significance.

Sweethearts

At five o'clock on a balmy May afternoon, Garland McKenney and her dog, Judy, scrambled down the levee to the backyard dock and into the family motorboat. Graduation was a week away and Clarence had something special planned for her at his fish camp deep in the bayou, where the Sweetheart River converged with the land. She was thrilled by the invitation. He'd never even shown the place to his wife. His innermost sanctum would soon be open to her.

It had been raining for weeks and the river was brown with tannin from the run-off upstream. Garland loved it like that—dark as a cup of brewed coffee. Against the solid blue of the sky, a quarter moon hung like a chalk mark.

She had been boating or swimming on this part of the Sweetheart all of her life. She knew it so well she could chart her progress in the shoreline's reflection—in the tree trunks laid out like submerged catwalks, the leafy treetops knitting together, then unraveling.

She reached a granddaddy cypress with the first bandanna (red for a left turn, blue for right, Clarence had said) and took the branch to Tate's Inlet, a familiar stretch dotted with floating fish camps. Trailing her hand in the water, she ticked off the structures fastened to rafts and barges as they bobbed into view: the abandoned A-frame infested with squirrels, the fake log cabin, the garish pink Victorian with gingerbread trim. After the last one disappeared around a curve, two blue bandannas appeared in quick succession. Two turns into twisting meanders, and she found herself on a part of the river she didn't recognize.

The creek narrowed into a choke of weeds. Garland ducked under a dense overhang of tupelo branches and cut the motor. In the sudden stillness, Judy, a muscular pit bull mix, snapped at a dragonfly and rose on her hind legs, poised to jump overboard. "Down, girl!" Garland commanded. Judy was a strong swimmer, but Garland knew that water moccasins and cottonmouths hunted in the sluggish shallows.

Just beyond the tangle of vegetation, the bow of a partially submerged john boat stuck out of the mud, the locals' version of a NO TRESPASSING sign. It was rumored that drug dealers and moonshiners strung steel wire across their creeks, that people had been slashed and even beheaded for venturing too far into the Sweetheart. She broke off a tupelo branch and waved it around, like a magician proving no strings were attached, then punched the motor and proceeded upstream. She looked at her watch: seven-thirty. It would be dark soon, and she had no idea how much farther the camp was.

For the next hour, pitch blackness was punctuated by the disembodied slurping and screeching of the swamp. She worried that she was lost, the thin beam of her flashlight a flimsy sword against the full armor of the night. To calm her nerves, she imagined the two of them cozy in the cabin, with only wild creatures for company. For the first time, they could truly relax without worrying that someone might see them together. Nothing was going to keep her from getting there.

At eight-forty P.M., nearly two hours later than Clarence had predicted, the deep yellow glow of windows lit by oil lamps shone through the miasma of the bayou. A cabin materialized around the yellow rectangles gradually, like a Polaroid picture developing. Garland cut the motor and paddled to the dock. Now that she had safely reached the cabin, she realized she'd have to spend the night and she hadn't even brought a toothbrush or Kibble for Judy. Worse, she'd have to concoct a lie for her father, Eastman, to explain why she had been out all night.

A screen door squealed open and Clarence appeared wearing a cap that said DON'T DO IT. "Where the hey have you been, Garland? I was worried."

"I've been to hell and back, just trying to get here." She secured the boat and signaled Judy forward with a click of her tongue. "You know I can't get home tonight. I'll have to make up a whopper for Eastman." She stepped onto the dock. An incipient growl issued from Judy's throat. Never completely at ease around the dog, Clarence fidgeted. "It's okay, girl." Garland tapped Judy lightly on the top of her head. "You said I'd get here by dusk." She waited for a response from Clarence. None came. "You lied to me. Why did you lie?"

He looked bereft. "I thought you wouldn't agree if I told you how far it was. God, I am so tired of the truck, the backseat of the car. We'll have privacy here."

"I don't like people making my decisions for me."

"Well, now you know where the place is and you can decide for yourself."

"Not tonight I can't." Anger coursed through her body, loosening her limbs. She thought she saw a flicker of light and peered into the bayou. "Where the fuck are we anyway, Georgia?"

Clarence bent over as if looking for something on the planks of the barge. "Did she say 'fuck'?" He was addressing his crotch.

"I'm serious, Clarence." Garland raised her hand to stop him from approaching, but a laugh crept into her voice and weakened her resolve. Judy pricked up her ears.

Clarence caught Garland's hand midair and rubbed it languidly against his cheek. His hand was large and square, sexy. Even his hand. Maybe there was something wrong with her, maybe she was a nymphomaniac. How could you tell? She was already picturing them horizontal, Clarence's face looming over hers, the hair on his chest teasing her skin until it felt like a million buds opening at once. She sighed and kissed his ear. Judy, a veteran to these scenes, lay down on the damp boards, her head between her outstretched paws.

Garland hadn't expected to have a serious boyfriend until she went to Florida State. Though it served the whole county, Sweetheart High was small—five hundred students. When you broke that down, it meant roughly 125 seniors and 62 boys. (She didn't count underclassmen.) Half the boys were black.

At Sweetheart High, blacks and whites danced and played sports together, but they rarely socialized. She would have gladly dated a black boy, if only to aggravate Eastman, who was the high school principal, but the opportunity hadn't materialized. She felt bad about that, especially considering how much she loved Carlene, the black housekeeper who had taken care of her for as long as she could remember. But Carlene herself would probably disapprove of a black boyfriend. Too complicated, she would say. Upset too many folks.

Because of Carlene, she didn't need as many friends as other girls. Also because of Judy. She loved Judy as much as she loved Carlene, and more than she loved Eastman. In fact, she didn't think she loved her father at all. How could you love someone who never loved you back? Eastman was her keeper, that was all. The only good thing he'd ever done was allow her to rescue a pup from the Tupelo County Animal Shelter for her tenth birthday. Garland worshipped the dog and spent the following summer training her. Judy grew into eighty-five pounds of chest with jaws like a bear trap. She was a sweet-tempered animal fond of crushing apples in a single chomp. She'd never bitten anyone, but people were careful how they moved and spoke around her. Garland took Judy along wherever she went.

Not that she was a loner. She had two girlfriends, Ina and Brittany. The three of them were brave together, and had twice gotten in trouble with the police: once for buying alcohol with a fake ID, and once for underage night driving. Though they were her best friends, from the first she decided not to tell them about Clarence. Neither girl could keep a secret, and besides, they might disapprove of her fooling around with a married man. They weren't grown up enough to understand misery the way Garland did. She had Eastman after all, day in and day out the very model of unhappiness, a man who had been in mourning for twelve years, ever since Garland's mother died.

━━

Following Clarence into his fish camp, Garland was greeted by a wall of trophies: two deer, a ring-tailed squirrel, a coyote, and a pheasant. Nothing, she thought, looked as dead as taxidermied animals. In place of quicksilver movements and eyes like falling stars, five dusty heads stared unblinking at nothing. Garland fingered the holster of Clarence's service revolver on the table by the door. "I don't think I could shoot an animal."

"I've seen you gut a fish with no problem. It's what you're used to. I've been hunting since I was nine."

Judy's ears shot up. She scrambled across the floor and began scratching at the wall.

"The dog's found the storage closet," Clarence said. "Bathroom's right over here." He pulled back a plastic curtain strung in front of a latrine. "Everything goes straight into the Sweetheart."

Garland cringed. The tides were so subtle this far back in the estuary, she had forgotten they were afloat on the river.

Clarence poured her a cup of champagne from an open bottle chilling in a galvanized bait bucket.

"Good," Garland muttered as she gulped it down. She

could feel the champagne immediately as the room swirled and settled, like a cast net. She began automatically to strip to her underwear. Judy, groaning with fatigue, coiled into an old wicker chair. Clarence's army cot was suddenly inviting, the sheet folded down over the drab blanket like a freshly ironed collar. "You know, the river just whipped me. And I'm starving."

Clarence placed a shrimp on her tongue and refilled her cup. She drained it, half noting a peculiar aftertaste. The room blurred again, this time without resolution, leaving broad brush strokes where there had been solid furniture. She was flattening out, becoming a picture of a girl. She reclined on the bed amid the streaks of color and passed out.

The next thing she saw was Clarence's shadow. Flung by a hurricane lamp, the bulging shape flowed toward her across the walls and ceiling, like an ink spill. She floated beneath it, buoyed up by hands under her buttocks, purring like a cat as he kissed her all over. Afterward, while he dozed, she watched the lamplight flicker across the fur and feathers of the dead animals until she drifted off. A door creaked or perhaps it slammed, and she turned in her sleep.

Garland had met Sheriff Clarence Coffey the previous November at a school assembly about drugs. From the third row of the auditorium, sandwiched between Ina and Brittany, she got a good look at him and decided on the spot that he was a double hunk with cherries on top.

Of course she recognized him. Everyone in Tupelo County

knew the sheriff, either in person or from the campaign posters plastered around the countryside in the last two elections. A star high school quarterback who'd married a cheerleader and gone to Vanderbilt on a football scholarship, he had always been something of a local celebrity. For the last four years, Garland had walked by the glass cabinet at school with the coronation portrait of him and his wife-to-be: the King and Queen of Senior Prom, Mr. Dick and Miss Dimple.

He was visiting the school to demonstrate the new narc dog, but first it was *this fried egg, your brain,* and so on. He presented himself as someone hip who knew a thing or two about drugs, but not firsthand. Pot, Sheriff Coffey claimed, was most perilous now for enticing teens to the real villains: Ecstasy, angel dust, crack, crystal meth, and even, he said, "what the Yankees call *horse.*" With a tad too much enthusiasm, he paraded a trunkful of confiscated bongs, spoons, hypodermics, rubber tourniquets, retorts, and tubing before the audience.

At last, he called the drug-sniffing dog and handler onto the stage. "This is Ralph, our new sniffer." He patted the German shepherd. The dog barked, eliciting laughs from the students.

The sheriff consigned the team out of sight, to the wings, and with a flourish befitting a performer, fished from the trunk six Baggies of grass identical to the dime bags Garland regularly bought from old man Hodges, her neighbor. He planted all but one of the bags in the auditorium, then asked for a volunteer. Ina grabbed Garland's arm and forced it into the air. "You there, the young lady down in front."

At least she looked decent that day: jeans, an orange scoop-neck top, matching orange Nikes. She had twisted her hair into a figure-eight chignon. Carlene had convinced her that she had the wrong coloring to wear silver jewelry so she was wearing new gold bead earrings and a gold chain that had belonged to her mother, an unexpected gift from Eastman.

As soon as Garland neared Clarence at the podium, she felt flustered and physically drawn to him, like an iron filing helplessly pulled toward a magnet. She recognized these sensations, but had never experienced them with such power and immediacy. When she was ten, and saw *A River Runs Through It,* she'd developed a crush on Brad Pitt. He played the younger, reckless brother who lived fast and died young. Her only boyfriend, Darryl Hainey, had been like that—brilliant, sullen, and defiant. Emotionally wounded in some unspoken way she had never understood but never doubted, Darryl mocked every conventional value. She was not attracted to happy boys, boys who planned to take over the family business, wherefore she had rejected the advances of Bill Lambert of Lambert's Food, Lester Chance of Chance Drugs, and Ned Harris of Harris's Feed and Seed.

The sheriff handed Garland the last Baggie. "Put it on your person—in your pocket, your socks—anywhere."

She nudged it under her ponytail elastic, then plumped her hair to conceal it.

"Very clever, young lady." Clarence shook her hand. His skin was hot and dry. Was she blushing? She held his hand a split-second too long. He must have noticed. Maybe everyone in the auditorium had noticed. Was this what people called "love at first sight"? It felt miserable.

She sat on stage with the faculty and principal, who eyed his daughter without expression. Typical. Eastman always acted as if she were just another of his charges, no one special, certainly not a blood relation. He had a wacky idea of fairness, believing it would be showing favoritism even to acknowledge her with a smile at school. She studied the floor.

The canine unit returned, the dog heeling precisely by his handler. "Everything is within one hundred feet," Clarence told the officer.

The dog rushed down the aisle, picking up scent, his tail like a whirligig propelling him. In short order, the team retrieved four bags under chairs and a fifth behind the dust-rimmed maroon stage curtain. As handler and dog turned smartly toward the people onstage, Garland thought she detected sweat beading up on the coach's forehead, but the dog passed him without incident. When he reached Garland, Ralph sat and barked, happily thumping his tail.

It always seemed to Garland that what happened next had happened without thought, almost involuntarily, as if her body had a mind of its own and could detach from her at will. She had removed the Baggie from her hair, but instead of dropping it into the sheriff's waiting palm, she had pocketed it, mugging broadly to the audience. The students hooted and whistled, stomped and hollered. When at last she relinquished the weed and curtsied, Sheriff Coffey was speechless. The assembly ended and this new, nervy Garland remained on the stage. "Can I pet the dog?"

"Sure. Ralph loves people." The sheriff took the leash from the handler and instructed the younger man to stow the drug paraphernalia in the Jeep parked outside. "What's your name?" He turned back toward her.

"Garland." She stroked the dog's glossy rump.

"Like a wreath?"

"Something like that." She hated being named after a singer who'd overdosed. If only her mother had named her for a fighter, someone like Sally Field. *Field McKenney*.

"You look familiar." He scratched Ralph's soft tan ruff.

"Maybe you've seen me with my father, Eastman McKenney, the principal."

"Of course." His hand stopped for a moment. "What's it like being the principal's daughter?"

"I don't know," Garland muttered. Could she sound any more insipid? Their hands collided in the dog's fur. "I hate it. It puts me in the spotlight, you know?"

"I can see that."

The dog swayed under their blithering hands, his eyes half-closed. Garland wanted to touch the papery warmth of the sheriff's hands, but fondled the dog's ears instead. "I'll vote for you next time you run. I'm old enough now," she volunteered. Oh, God, that was *so* suck-uppy.

He looked directly into her eyes then and it felt like the sun had emerged from behind a cloud. "Thanks, young lady."

"I'm not a laaady," Garland protested, pulling at the word until it was *Gone with the Wind*.

"Oh? Then what are you?" He sounded annoyed.

"I'm a woman. A young woman."

"Same thing, isn't it?"

"Nope. A young ledda wayas bonnets and has impeccable mannuhs." He looked blankly at her. She turned off the accent. "While a woman is anatomically correct." She was proud of her composure, but he made a sour face and turned to leave, yanking the dog behind him.

Crap. She had screwed up. He wasn't used to bold flirting. Neither was she. Until now, her rebelliousness had not included men or sex. She hadn't trusted her body to anyone except Darryl Hainey one inept time, so inept that while she was glad to have jumped the hurdle of virginity, she sensed that she had missed something.

"The important thing is that you're female," the sheriff called back over his shoulder. And then he had winked.

The next Friday, as she left Lambert's grocery, a police car with its lights silently flashing eased around the corner and rolled to a stop alongside her. She peered in the open window. He said, "I thought that was you."

"Oh, hi," she managed.

"That sack looks heavy. Can I give you a ride?"

She handed him the parcel and climbed in. She wanted to speak, but nothing came to mind.

She had noticed patrol cars on the street everywhere over the last week. To no avail, she had driven by the police station at least five times hoping for a glimpse of him. She had felt a little ashamed stalking him, but mostly she was intoxicated by the possibilities.

They drove past her car in the grocery's parking lot. She would have to lie about that; she'd say she left the car at the store because she'd flooded it.

She suspected he knew her address, but when he asked for it, she gave it to him. They rode in silence, her breathing finally normal.

He stopped short of the house, located on five wooded acres of riverfront at the end of a dirt road. The nearest neighbor, old man Hodges, was a retired tobacco farmer whose acreage lay fallow thanks to federal tobacco subsidies. The McKenneys rarely saw or heard him through the trees.

The sheriff turned to her. "I'd like to know you better. I feel—"

"Me too," she said, calling up all her courage.

He reached for her hand. Her jitters coalesced into lightning wherever his fingers rested.

"I want to show you something," he said.

Oh God, don't let him take off his clothes! She had imagined him naked all week, but now she didn't want him to disrobe. She sucked in her breath.

"Have you ever seen the shell mound on the bay?"

"What?"

"You know, where the university is digging for Indian artifacts?"

She knew the place, a garbage heap of thousand-year-old oyster and clam shells. "I might have been there as a baby." Wasn't there a snapshot in the family album of her and her mother taken in front of an indistinct white heap? *Lorelei and Garland at the shell mound, September 17, 1985.*

"I'd like to show it to you tomorrow."

"All right."

———

He wasn't wearing his uniform for the outing on Saturday. Both sported sunglasses and hats. So we don't have to see each other's faces, Garland thought; so we can pretend this is perfectly ordinary, two people out for an afternoon ride.

The shell mound lay at the western edge of Sweetheart Bay, at the end of a three-mile washboard road canopied with live oak trees. On either side, vegetation striped with dried mud crowded in. As Clarence talked about the dig, alternating bands of sunlight and shade passed over them in the Jeep like the flickering of a giant film projector. The head archeologist was an old friend from Vanderbilt. A year ago, he had told Clarence, a graduate student probing for pottery shards had unearthed a foundation stone. Infrared photographs confirmed the outline of an old Spanish mission church and two smaller buildings.

Clarence parked and they exited, leaving the mechanical purr of the engine for the thrum and caw of the animals of the Florida Panhandle. Overhead, a turkey vulture floated in slow circles, the tips of its wing feathers soft rudders in the thermal updraft.

They made their way down a narrow path bordered on one side by a high chain-link fence. Behind it, the white dome of the mound glared in the afternoon sun. They brushed past scrub oaks, palmettos, wild indigo, and orange swatches of poison ivy. Garland pointed to a trailer ahead of them. Someone had painted the word MARGARITAVILLE along with cartoons of glasses, limes, and a salt shaker on the white aluminum siding.

"I've got the keys to the kingdom," Clarence said, loping ahead to unlock the door.

There wasn't a spare inch in the mobile home, which was packed like a traveling museum with boxes of artifacts, tools, journals, reference books, and a computer array. Clarence retrieved two cans of Diet Coke from a small refrigerator. Together, they sorted through the boxes, examining stone axes, arrowheads, Timucuan pottery shards with fine decorations like bird footprints, and other historical tatters.

"Okay," Clarence said. "Time to see the real treasure. Are you ready for her?"

"Her?"

"Yes, it's definitely a woman," Clarence said. "You'll see."

Once, on TV, Garland had seen an archeologist handling partial skulls dug from the torrid hills of East Africa. Maybe Clarence's friend had found a woman's femur or a jawbone in the sand of Florida.

They left the trailer and followed a footpath into the scrub. Palmetto fronds and switch cane plucked at Garland's trousers as she breezed past. In a few minutes, they reached a rectangular pit staked off with orange tape. A white boat ladder protruded from the hole.

"We have to go down one at a time," Clarence said. "Don't touch anything."

He went first to make sure the ladder was steady. When he reached the bottom, he pulled back a blue tarp. "Amazing," he called up. Garland peered after him, but it was too dark to see anything from above.

Clarence climbed out and watched intently as she descended.

Over the years, Garland had found mice and lizard bones in owl pellets, but she had never seen a human bone. Now a complete skeleton glimmered faintly in the dirt, the rib cage rising in graceful curves as if still inflated by breath.

"She's a Potano," Clarence said. "They think there was a graveyard here."

The woman lay in her grave without benefit of a coffin, or perhaps the wood had disintegrated in half a millennium. She looked peaceful, lying on her back in the Christian burial position, arms penitently crossed at her chest. Garland could easily picture the owner of the waxy yellow bones swimming in the river, collecting dyestuffs, carrying water in a clay jug. Her skull had held thoughts and desires, intuitions and the rudiments of math and logic. She would have felt hunger and thirst. But would she have imagined another woman staring at her bones centuries later?

"What do you think?"

"God," she said, moved to tears. "I think we are like everyone who has ever lived."

When she climbed out Clarence was beaming. "It's moving, isn't it?" He wiped his forehead with his sleeve.

"Yes, it is."

"I don't want to sound corny, but you make me feel that same way."

"What way?"

He scuffed a clean patch on the ground and sat down. "As if I'm looking at something rare, something precious." He patted the dirt beside him.

"You think I'm precious?" She knelt, then sat next to him, the cold of the ground quickly permeating her jeans.

"You might be, to me." He took her hand in both of his. "I'm married, of course you know that."

His serious tone scared her. Did he think she was looking for a husband? If they had been the same age, she thought, she probably wouldn't have found him interesting. "Of course I do. That's one of the things I like about you, didn't you know?"

He laughed and hugged her close, enveloping her in his body heat, kissing her neck and mouth.

She thought she might faint. But the pleasure merely amplified as he traced circles over her breast. Warmth suffused her and something deep within began to soften. Now his hand was inside her shirt. They lay back on his canvas barn coat, which he had somehow removed and placed beneath her. A moment later, she felt his other hand reach inside her underwear, and then she felt herself contract around his finger. Was that an orgasm? He continued to move his hand inside her, slowly inserting and withdrawing three fingers, easily now. She made a sound she had never heard before, reached for him, and held on. Long, blue-gray shadows began to fill up the woods around them, like water rising from an invisible spring. Overhead, oak branches crisscrossed in a slow frenzy. He fumbled with a rubber, then entered her. They rocked together slowly, and then he came, grunting, his breath hot in her ear and on her face. It was some kind of miracle, she had no idea, no idea.

They were true, all the songs and stories: afterward, she was different. Even that first night Carlene noticed it. "You look like you're sleepwalking," she said as Garland bent to the sideboard to refill her dinner plate. Garland suspected that Carlene hadn't believed the story about the car abandoned at the grocery store the day before. Eastman had. He always believed her lies until he was forced to discard them. He didn't want to know the truth.

She thought of nothing but the sheriff. She dreamed about him at night and daydreamed during waking hours. She decided not to contact him. The silence between them was not a lack; it grew heavy and palpable, like the air in a heated room. The temperature rose the longer they stayed apart.

She thought about sex continuously. She fantasized she was a deer and he a stag and they leapt in synchrony in the woods, then bounded off in different directions. She fantasized she was a rare Florida panther and he was the lone, prowling male—nocturnal, musky, with luminous eyes and bubble-gum pink lips. She was embarrassed and excited all the time and blushed at her own thoughts. Darryl Hainey had never made her feel this way.

Two days passed. The next evening, when he called, Carlene answered, then handed Garland the telephone. He didn't waste time on small talk; maybe he was within eavesdropping range. "Next Saturday, four o'clock. Behind the post office."

"All right," she said.

She had been alone with him twice and would have done anything to see him a third time. Thus began their clandestine life, a life marked as much by caution as by risk and thrill. She agreed to whatever he suggested, yielding to his greater age and experience. Yielding to the heat. Being with him was like drugs, like getting drunk or stoned, the world expanding around her and then contracting to fit inside her head.

For the first time she was grateful for her body. Admiring her reflection in the full-length mirror on her bedroom door, she touched herself, pretending to be him. Her body had come alive for him like a plucked string, like a fish returned to water. That was the gift he had bestowed on her. Before, she was a puzzle of many pieces, smooth and sharp-edged, differently textured and hued. He had touched her and made the skin and organs and nerve endings combine into a magnificent creature that answered to the name *Garland*.

———

Over the next four delirious months, she ignored her schoolwork. At first, her grades dropped; on her spring midterm report she barely had a B-minus average. Eastman warned that her acceptance at FSU would be jeopardized if she didn't maintain her grades through senior year. Though she couldn't imagine herself two hours away in Tallahassee, a monotonous inner voice periodically cajoled her to read, hand in papers, study for exams. She obeyed, oddly able to concentrate in sporadic bursts. Her work improved: love had made her smarter.

Ina and Brittany complained they never saw her anymore. She fobbed them off with tales of studying long hours, being grounded for minor infractions, car trouble.

Usually she and Clarence got stoned and sometimes they drank. He called the shot of Jim Beam or Rebel Yell on top of the joint "polishing his head." It improved the sex, he said, and prolonged the high. Maybe it was why he paid attention to every part of her, including her feet and ears.

Though they had never run into anyone they knew, Clarence was paranoid about being recognized, so they avoided anywhere civilized or public—no motels, movies, restaurants, not even the malls in Pensacola or Tallahassee. They spent their time together in the wilderness, in his boat or tent, in the back of his Jeep.

Only Carlene was suspicious; one day she almost wormed it out of Garland. "You've become a nature lover," Carlene commented, pointing to Garland's linen slacks as she sorted the laundry on the back porch.

Garland eyed the white pants smeared with mud and grass. "Bird watching," she said without missing a beat.

"Looks more like you were sitting on the birds."

"That's gross, Car."

"I noticed a button missing on your pink blouse last week." She dropped some towels into the washer.

"Gee, I didn't."

"That's because I sewed on the spare one. Plus you're making much more dirty clothes."

"I admit it; I'm going out on dates. Satisfied?"

Carlene lowered the lid of the washing machine. She frowned. "Why didn't you tell me, honey?"

"I don't know. I'm older now," Garland said. "It's no big deal, anyway. I hardly know the person."

"A boy at school?"

Garland coughed and leaned over the sink to drink from the tap. She pretended to have forgotten the question.

"What's his name?"

"I'd rather not say at this point."

"He's not at your school, is he?" Sometimes Carlene could read Garland's mind.

"I met him at school, so don't get off on the wrong track," Garland sniped back. "Don't be too sure of yourself, Sherlock."

"I just hope he's worthy of you."

"I don't really think it's your business. I mean, you're not my mother."

Carlene dropped her gaze and stepped back a little, as if someone had poked her in the chest.

"Anyhow, it's not as if I'm getting married. We're just going out." Sometimes Carlene went too far. There was a time when Garland confided everything in her, but that was before Garland grew up. Carlene didn't seem to have noticed until just this minute.

Carlene lodged the laundry basket under one bony arm, opened the porch door, and reentered the house. "You just watch yourself, you hear?"

Garland grabbed a pile of sheets and towels and followed her.

Carlene stopped on the stairs. "You're not as high and mighty as you think, Garland. I don't care if you don't listen to me, but you better listen to somebody who knows more than you do."

Right, Garland thought. And who would that be? There wasn't one person in the whole town other than Clarence who understood her now. "Uh-huh. Actually, this person is more like a friend than a boyfriend. And he knows a lot."

"You'd best remember what I always told you: men will promise you anything but they give you about six inches."

Two days later, parked with Clarence by the river, Garland produced Curious George, dangling the old stuffed toy monkey by his tail. "Swear on George you'll always be my friend, no matter what."

"What brought this on?"

"Carlene's been hassling me. She's suspicious."

Clarence looked alarmed.

"Oh, not of you. Of me."

"Why would you care about what an old black woman says?"

"Just swear on George you'll always be my friend."

"Whatever you want, Sweetheart. I swear on George."

"Don't call me 'Sweetheart,' please. The town just ruins it for me. I hate this place."

"Well, I love it. And you ought to love it, too," Clarence said, turning serious. "It's your home. It has a rich history."

She knew the history. It was drummed into every kid in the

county. Grits and chintz, bullets and chicory, gambling and whores: that's what the antebellum steamboats carried up and down the Sweetheart. Very colorful, but she still hated it. There probably wasn't another person in the world who lived in a town called Sweetheart but had never been loved. It was a cruel joke. "Anyway, you have to kiss George when you swear on him."

Clarence rolled his eyes. "This is stupid."

"Just do it, Sheriff. Pucker up."

"All right." He quickly pressed the monkey's face to his own, smacking loudly.

"Did you actually touch fuzz?" she asked. "With your tongue?"

In April, they finally had a chance to be alone together in a house. Clarence's archeologist friend was vacationing and had given Clarence the use of his home. Though Garland couldn't sleep over, they'd have two afternoons and evenings together indoors, a first.

Garland felt skittish, even illicit in the house. She wondered how much Clarence had told his friend about her. She didn't like the idea of someone she had never met knowing her secrets.

While Clarence arranged groceries in the refrigerator and fiddled with the hot tub, Garland explored the wife's clothes, the cool silk squares of a scarf drawer, a bouquet of embroidered panties in ice cream colors. She was getting tired of having to sneak around to be with Clarence.

She found a filmy black slip on a hanger and decided to take it. In return, she tucked her red thong underwear in the sleeve of a heavy woolen coat that smelled of mothballs. The wife wouldn't find them unless she traveled north or Sweetheart had one of its rare cold snaps. Either way, she'd blame her husband, maybe even divorce him. Garland halfway liked the idea.

The floating fish camp rocked her awake. Or was it the whispering? Though she couldn't understand the words, she grasped secrecy and intimacy from the faint chatter and hiss.

Her eyes opened upon Clarence and a strange woman standing near the latrine, sipping from plastic cups. The woman was grinning under heavy makeup and blond hair moussed into sprockets. She was older than Garland, maybe older than Clarence.

"Are you awake?" Clarence was asking Garland, perched on the narrow margin of the bed. When he placed his hand on her belly, she flinched.

"I guess so."

He waved the stranger closer. "This is an old friend of mine, Shelley."

"I feel like I know you already," the woman said.

Suddenly aware she was half-naked, Garland tugged the sheet up to her neck. "Excuse me, I'd like to get dressed."

Shelley turned her back while Garland jammed on her clothes. "So what's the plan?" she asked, straightening the bed.

"We're having a party," Clarence said. Shelley chuckled.

She poured herself a shot of Rebel Yell from a bottle tucked behind the cooler.

"I think you two got a head start on me." Garland wanted to sound confident, but inside, she was queasy and confused. She checked her watch: one A.M. She looked out the window. In the faint spill of light from the cabin, two boats—hers and Clarence's—rocked in the current, chipping at the silver-edged ripples. Shelley must have been there the whole time.

Clarence brought her a cup of wine. He smelled like whiskey mixed with the ladies' room at the local Italian restaurant. "It's your graduation present." He dropped his voice. "We'll all party together. It'll be real nice." As if on cue, Shelley stepped forward and put an arm around Garland.

Garland shuddered. She looked to the trophies on the wall: the animals stared straight ahead, like helpless children in the midst of a family fight.

"Nice titties," Shelley sang, sticking out her chest and pivoting like a runway model. She turned and bent forward. "Nice firm ass."

"Knock if off, Shelley," Clarence said.

"I'm drunk," the woman explained.

"You're revolting," Garland said. She immediately wanted to take it back. Her anger scared her: What would she do or say next? And how could Clarence think she wanted this? He should have asked her first. Now it was too late. Everything was ruined.

"She's no fun," Shelley complained.

"Come on, Garland, calm down." He drew her toward him and whispered in her ear. "It's just for kicks. It doesn't mean anything. It's you I love. Shelley's just your toy for the night."

"I think she's your toy." She'd been waiting for him to use the word "love." Now he had and she didn't believe him. It was amazing how someone you thought you loved could change all at once. Or was it that the person stayed the same and the love disappeared? Either way, the result was a terrible sense of emptiness.

"Drink your wine like a good girl." Shelley raised her cup as if to toast.

Without knowing she was going to, Garland dumped her wine on Shelley.

"Bitch!" the woman cried. Clarence glared at Garland as he blotted Shelley's blouse with a napkin.

Garland backed up toward the door, until she bumped into the table, where she felt Clarence's weapon poke her waist. Oh yes, the gun. She lifted it out of the holster and brandished it in the air. Did it have a safety? How did it work? Judy, ensconced in the chair, lifted her head. "Up, good girl," she commanded, and the dog sprang to her side. Clarence and Shelley cowered at the foot of the bed.

"Leave," Garland said. The hand holding the gun wavered slightly, like seaweed hanging in water.

Clarence moved toward her. "Stop it this minute, you little cunt. You might hurt somebody."

Garland steadied the gun with her other hand and raised it. "Open the door and get out."

It was so easy with the gun. She could make them do whatever she wanted. Shelley and Clarence scurried past. "Watch them!" she told Judy. Showing her teeth and growling, the dog herded them to the edge of the dock. "Get in the boat," Garland ordered from the doorway. With the back of her hand, she wiped at the hot tears blurring her vision.

The pair climbed in and huddled together.

"Leave, you idiots!"

They started the motor and disappeared into the mist, Clarence yelling obscenities. "You're going to be good and sorry," he roared. "Sorry" trailed off like the end of a song on the radio.

She returned to the cabin, ate a few shrimp, drank half a bottle of wine, and fell asleep, Judy curled beside her on the bed. When she woke at first light, she removed the trophy animals from the wall and lowered them respectfully into the river. Then, working in a stinging pall of mosquitoes and no-see-ums, she doused the cabin with gasoline from a can on the dock, and set it ablaze. Navigating the creeks to the mainstream, she could smell the tarry stench of burning pine for hours.

Eastman was eating breakfast when Garland returned. "You look like hell," he said, lifting a spoonful of grits to his mouth. Carlene shouted hello from the next room. She didn't seem to know Garland had been out all night.

"I got lost. It was awful."

"You okay, honey?" Carlene stepped into the kitchen.

"Yeah, I'm good." Garland draped her arms around her father's neck. He didn't budge. "I'm so glad to be home." A brilliant ploy, she thought: act loving and needy.

He set his coffee cup down and patted her twice on the hand. "Where were you?"

"On the river."

"All night?"

"I decided to go for a ride in the afternoon. I went past Tate's Inlet and got lost. I slept in the boat. It was scary." She sniffled.

Carlene said, "Even black folks know not to mess in there."

"Carlene," Eastman said, "could you do the bedrooms first today?" Carlene made a face behind his back and lugged her vacuum up the back stairway.

"I'm starving," Garland said, sounding as helpless as she could.

"There are eggs available on the refrigerator door."

She wanted to grab her father and shake him. Why didn't he fuss over her, smooth back her hair from her forehead, fix her an omelet? Why must he always sound like an announcement for produce at Winn Dixie?

"Are you sure you were alone?" Eastman avoided looking at her.

"Why do you always think I'm lying? What have I ever done to you, Dad, directly to you?"

He paused to think. "You've stomped on my heart." He dropped some papers into his briefcase and snapped it shut. The chair scraped against the floor. His suited back retreated through the doorway, brown and wrinkled. "You could have left a note." He turned to face her from the next room. "I was up half the night worrying you were dead in a ditch somewhere."

"Does that mean you love me, Eastman? Is that your version of 'I love you'? How touching, how totally touching."

━━━

The big loss in the fire was a stash of marijuana worth $50,000, or so Clarence claimed in a phone call. "Damn you to hell, Garland McKenney," he had said, and slammed down the phone.

Eastman knew nothing except that she had been gone all night without a good explanation and that was enough for him to mourn his dead wife again for weeks.

Shortly after the fire, Judy disappeared. She had never gone missing in all her eight years. Garland enlisted Carlene, old man Hodges, Ina, and Brittany to search, but there wasn't a trace. No one had seen her on the road to the river.

On Friday, Garland found Judy's body in a thick spot in the water at the end of the dock. It was the first place she'd looked initially, worried that the dog might have slipped off the levee, knocked herself out, and drowned. The vet said she had probably been poisoned. Garland was certain that someone had kidnapped and killed Judy, then returned her body so Garland would find it.

She would have wept for weeks but Judy's death so terrified her that like a rabbit under the gaze of a predator, she froze. Later, she told herself. She would mourn Judy later. In the meantime, she had to leave Sweetheart. It was one thing not to be loved and quite another to be hated.

Dear Carlene,

The man I was going out with has betrayed me. I'm sure he's the one who killed Judy. I just can't live here anymore. Eastman has no clue. I told him that I was going with Ina to visit her aunt in New Jersey for a week (as you know). But I'm not coming back. I'll have a phone soon, and I'll call you. I'll miss you, Car. Don't worry.

Love always,
Garland

Carlene collects this note in her mail from the rickety stand of boxes at the corner of Harrier Lane and Highway 232. It is late June and the sky is still bright though it's close to eight-thirty. Carlene likes the long days of summer. She didn't go north like her siblings because she can't abide cold weather and short, dreary days.

She reads the letter standing at the kitchen sink, glancing between sentences through the kitchen window crowded with sweet potato vines and a philodendron that has climbed on sticky pod feet to the ceiling and nearly encircles the room.

She has always worried about Garland and nearly every one of her worries has come true in one way or another. She reads the letter twice, then tucks it into a kitchen drawer that holds her important papers. (She had planned to buy a desk, but what would she really *do* at a desk besides pay the light bill?) She hangs her purse on a hook and climbs the stairs to her bedroom, changes into a housecoat, and lies down on top of the bedspread.

Carlene had scrupulously avoided commenting on Garland's trip, even when Eastman repeated Garland's lie every night that week while she served him dinner. She was suspicious it was no vacation from the start, though the girl hadn't confided in her and she'd quit asking her questions. But Carlene knew that Garland had taken the quilt her mother made her. It must have filled up her whole suitcase.

Carlene has known Garland since the day she found her playing house, a six-year-old crouched under a dining table overhung with a sheet. Garland's mother had been dead for three months. From that day on, Carlene has been the McKenneys' housekeeper. She has cleaned the house, babysat Garland, done the laundry and shopping, and cooked dinner five nights a week.

Carlene vividly recalls entering the rambler for the first time, meeting Mr. McKenney, a sad, formal man. She was thirty-eight then and determined not to be a substitute mother, or worse yet, some sort of mammy. After all, it was 1989. Even in Sweetheart, Florida, there were enough registered black voters to elect more than the token commissioner and just the year before they had elected three.

Of course Carlene fell in love with Garland. How could she not? The child had all the charms of a six-year-old and some unique enticements as well—a disarming capacity for laughter and a talent for mimicking the way other people walked and talked. How many times had Carlene nearly fallen down laughing just when she was trying to discipline the child? How many times had she wanted to take her home after work, install her in the tiny spare bedroom in the attic for a weekend or a week? But Eastman McKenney was not a man who would have allowed such intimacy, even if Carlene had been white, even if she had been a relative. Eastman's sister had stayed in the house following the funeral to look after Garland. As soon as he could arrange it, Eastman had hired Carlene and sent his sibling back to her peanut farm in Georgia.

The phone rang and rang. Carlene answered, fuzzily, on the eighth ring.

"It's me, Garland."

"I know it's you."

"How are you, lovey-dovey?" That was Garland's oldest pet name for Carlene.

"I'm fine. What about you? Is everything okay?"

"I've got a problem, actually."

"A new one, there in New Jersey?"

"New York. I've moved to New York City."

Carlene sat up on the bed.

"I'm sorry to call and lay it on you."

"It's all right, Sweetheart. I want to hear all about it."

Crash Course

A few years before Williamsburg, Brooklyn, was restored to its present chic incarnation, while it still slumbered in blighted ruin, Abby Presner found herself driving there on a street with more potholes than macadam. She was headed for the Williamsburg community pool, a once-elegant natatorium that had fallen on hard times like the rest of the neighborhood. She had swum in it the previous year on her annual trip to New York and remembered graffiti scrawled across patchy mosaic walls and a locker room as dank as the inside of a bucket. Still, she had to go. At fifty-five, the only way she could control her back pain was to swim at least every other day. Her friend Esther had drawn a map of the three-mile route to the pool. It lay beside her on the front seat of Esther's car.

Turning right on North Berry, she found herself on an avenue of small storefronts painted in garish combinations of red, black, and yellow. There were few people around, even though it was early evening and not yet dark. She came to a stop sign, dutifully applied the brakes, then crept forward. The next thing she knew, a large black mass was ramming into her front end, sending her car sliding sideways. Metal squealed on metal; headlamp glass rained down. A black Lincoln Continental inched down the block before finally coming to a halt.

She took a deep breath and leaned back to collect herself. She didn't think she was hurt; both cars had been traveling slowly. But from the sound of it, the fender had been sheared off.

The other driver, a young man, was already appraising the damage. There was no other traffic. A few customers rushed out of a corner bodega and stood staring at the accident from afar.

Abby unstrapped herself and carefully climbed from the low-slung car. "I guess we should call the police," she shouted to the young man standing in the street with both hands on his hips, shaking his head. He snickered and said something in Spanish to a second man, who, Abby thought, judging by his fawning body language, must be his underling.

"Excuse me," Abby began again, walking toward him. "I guess we ought to call the police so we can get an accident report number. This isn't my car—"

"Are you crazy, lady?" the young man bellowed.

Abby was close enough now to see his face: handsome, well groomed, perhaps in his mid-twenties. He had a swagger even standing still. His friend sniffed the air, shifting his weight from foot to foot.

"Nobody's calling the police. That's not how we do things in this part of town," the young man said.

Though long ago Abby had lived in New York for a decade, she had never ventured far into Brooklyn. The performances she attended now when she visited to gather ideas for the

Abby Presner Dance Studio were all held in Manhattan. Still, Brooklyn wasn't a foreign country, just a borough. "You always have to call the police in an accident," she argued. "I need your insurance information and you need mine. That's why people have insurance, so they don't have to pay out of their own pocket."

"Me pay? You *are* crazy. She's crazy, 'Lipe," he told his companion. "Call the police? Hah! What are you on?"

"Excuse me?"

"Angel dust." He jutted his chin forward and back, as if keeping time to a song. "I bet you're on angel dust."

"Look, you hit me and I had the right of way."

"We both had stop signs."

"True, but I was on your right. You were supposed to yield to me," Abby explained.

"I don't yield to nobody."

"This is not my car. It belongs to a friend." She always stayed with Esther, her oldest friend, a struggling painter who for thirty years had been an unwilling trailblazer for real estate developers, moving from one unsavory, Bohemian neighborhood to another as gentrification raised rents. Abby regarded the detached fender and crumpled hood of Esther's pitiful car. Blotches of rust floated like islands in a sea of blue body paint. "You were at fault, so your insurance will have to fix it."

"That piece of shit?" He kicked the driver's door of the Toyota Starlet and muttered a string of curses in Spanish.

Fear fluttered briefly in her chest, then vanished. The accident was his fault and he should pay for the damage to

Esther's car even if it was a piece of shit built to be marketed in the Third World.

"I own this corner," the young man announced.

"This is his corner," said 'Lipe, spreading his arms apart. "In all directions."

The young man scanned the intersection. "*Hola,* we need to move the cars," he said. "We're blocking traffic." He snapped his fingers and 'Lipe hurried to relieve him of his car keys, then hopped into the long, black car and pulled it to the curb.

Abby painstakingly folded herself back into the Toyota and turned the key. The two men had a refined system of communication, like a dance duo. 'Lipe was the gofer, the sidekick, devoted friend. She could not imagine anyone she knew being so completely at her disposal. They were like a pair of dancers in a pas de deux. 'Lipe did the light lifting and his boss the heavy lifting.

She parked the car behind 'Lipe and climbed out. "I'll be right back," she called as she trudged to the corner bodega with its red-and-yellow awning. They followed her without a word. "I'd like to use your phone," she told the short, balding man at the counter. Over her shoulder, she sensed the pair looming in the doorway, smirking.

The bodega owner glanced at the men, then studied the floor. "Phone is no working."

"I see." She turned to go. The two men blocked her path. "All right," she said. "No phone call."

"You have a cell phone? Pager?"

"Nope." She could already hear her husband's harangue.

Now do you understand why you need a cell phone? She hated electronic gadgets. She was just learning email.

"Let me see."

She held her purse open as he peered in and poked at the contents with one finger.

"Who are you?" he asked.

"My name is Abby."

"Abby, Abby." He drew the name through his lips, tasting it like a piece of licorice. "You live around here?"

"I'm visiting from Florida."

"Oh," he said knowingly. "Cubana."

She thought for a moment. "Let's just say I'm a brown woman." *In the future, we will all be brown or there won't be a future.* She had worked in the Civil Rights movement in the early seventies. That was how she thought of herself, though today Brown had a capital "B" and meant Hispanic.

"A *brown* woman? You *are* crazy."

"Look, I need to get to the pool, so I'm going to leave, okay? I have a bad back, that's why I swim." Maybe if he knew she was in pain, he would rise to the occasion and do the right thing. "If you don't want to call the police, give me some money to fix my friend's car." She was willing to settle for almost any amount just to resolve the situation. "A hundred would be good."

"I don't care about your friend. I don't care about you or your backache." He and 'Lipe laughed. "Tell me one reason I should care." He looked pensive.

"I'm a human being."

"Next reason."

"Look, pretty soon, the pool is going to close and I'll miss my chance."

"You are not going anywhere. She's on something, eh, 'Lipe?"

"I am not on anything."

"If you're not fucked up on something, then you're just plain whacked." His voice was lighter, more casual. "Come on, people are staring. Let's go sit down and I'll explain to you about the cops." He began walking toward his car. She followed at a short distance.

He opened the door of the Lincoln Continental. Inside, everything was black velvet with the exception of a plush pink mouse, like a cat's toy, which dangled from the rearview mirror. A gold cardboard crown on the dashboard leaked sweet deodorizer.

The young man got in behind the wheel. 'Lipe opened the passenger door for Abby and then got into the back. She sat on the front seat, leaving her door ajar. The young man angled his body sideways and slouched against his door to face her.

She wondered if she should have gotten into the car. She was too trusting, always had been. Esther had described this neighborhood as a vibrant mix of hookers and poets, gallery owners and shoplifters. She hadn't called it dangerous. On the other hand, Abby knew that the character of the city changed block by block.

He turned the ignition key until the dashboard illuminated, switched off the radio, closed the electric windows, and turned on the air conditioner. Her door was still open.

"I'm a drug dealer, lady," he whispered. "And this is my corner. Naturally I don't want the police around."

"I see," Abby said. She was aware of her mind churning, as if it were crushing ice. "You know, now that we are talking so personally, I have to say that I'm not comfortable in the car. Please don't take it the wrong way." She held his gaze, unblinking. "It's just that I don't know you well. You probably wouldn't get into a stranger's car either, would you?"

"You really are loco, Abby." It was the first time he had used her name since she'd given it to him in the bodega, and it both pleased and alarmed her, as if he had learned something deeply private about her. "Okay, 'Lipe, help her out."

For a split second she worried that this was some sort of code, that 'Lipe would slam her door shut, but he merely offered his arm as she exited onto the curb.

The trio stood in the street, as restless as three snakes.

The young man lit a cigarette. "You should be afraid of me. I know you are. That's why I let you out of the car." He inhaled, exhaled. "You know, I don't give a shit about anything. I could cut your face. I could kill someone if I needed to." He blew smoke at her. She fanned it away.

Abby wasn't going to be intimidated or treat this nameless young man any differently from anyone else. Wasn't that the heart of acceptance? Expecting more from people? "What are you doing here, anyway?" she asked, out of the blue.

"What do you mean what am *I* doing here? I live here. The question is what are *you* doing here? Go back to Florida. You are so nuts. I bet you're on angel dust. You smoke weed?"

"I used to. I'm too old now. I smoke it maybe once a year." Even with the body and posture of a dancer, Abby realized that to the young man, she probably looked like someone's grandmother.

"I think you're on something. You're high," he declared again.

"No, I'm not. Look, why do you live here? Have you ever lived anywhere else?"

"Who wants to know?"

"I have a son your age. You ought to try living somewhere else. The whole country is not like New York."

"You have kids?"

"Two."

He could have been one of her children. He had the same olive skin and dark hair. Her chest ached just thinking about this possibility. "And you?"

"Are you nuts? Do I look like the Dagwood type?"

"You read *Blondie*?"

He scuffed at the ground. "What makes you think I care about you? I don't care about anything. I'm probably going to be dead before I'm thirty," he said flatly.

"You really should go somewhere else." An image popped into her mind, pristine and vivid. He stood in a back bay fishing craft wearing a white captain's cap with a shiny black visor. He was joking with wealthy customers, bursting into Spanish as a client hooked a big fish. "You could be a fishing boat captain."

He was silent for a moment, trying to get the idea into his

head, Abby hoped. "You are the craziest woman I have ever met. I don't want to go somewhere else. I like it here."

"You *like* it here?"

He nodded definitively.

"What does that mean? That you're used to it? How do you know if you've never been anywhere else? I mean, you're not a plant. You could move. You could go to Paris, London, Miami, Chicago."

'Lipe couldn't help himself; he started to giggle. "You're a tree, man, and you didn't even know it."

She had the strong impulse to invite him home, to save him. This, she knew, was plain old hubris. Besides, it was dangerous to believe you could save a person with the force of your personality. A friend of hers, a college professor, had been shot by a graduate student he was trying to save. But she believed that her young man was salvageable. If only he had a relative in another part of the country, like Nebraska, someplace with clean air, open spaces, food growing in the ground. "You could make a good living as a boat captain and you'd live to be a fat old man."

"Are you saying I'm fat? Jesus, you are totally nuts. Angel dust nuts. I seen people on angel dust, and you are it. Maybe Ecstasy."

"Come to Florida. Just try it. Take a vacation to St. Petersburg and go out on a fleet fishing boat. You could also make good money in construction. An enterprising young man like you would do well because the state is growing fast. My husband builds houses and he's—"

"Do I give a shit about your husband?" He yelled it. "Don't waste my time. Look, Florida is not cool. New York is cool."

'Lipe said, "New York is it."

The young man stepped directly in front of her. "Why are you butting your nose in my business? It's not your business where I live, what I do. What do you do, Miss Know It All? Do you even work, you crazy *brown* woman?"

"I'm a reporter," she said, amazed by her instantaneous duplicity.

"Really?" He stepped back, as if stunned by a blow. "You write about people for the news?"

"Yeah. You know, you look like my son." She wanted to switch the subject before he caught her in the lie. She touched his arm, held it for a second for emphasis. She felt his body respond, as if they were characters in a fairy tale and could change each other with a touch.

"You're really a writer? You're not shitting me?" His whole demeanor changed. His face and voice softened. He suddenly found her interesting. "I have a lot of stories," he said, his tone now childlike. "You could write a book about a person like me. I've had such a . . . a . . . such an exciting life, *verdad*."

"*Verdad*," 'Lipe concurred.

"You'd tell me your stories?"

"Look at this!" He tapped her arm, then rolled up a pant leg. "You see this?"

Inked on his calf was a grotesque tattoo, demons snarling amid droplets of blood and serpents intertwining to make a curlicued border. "You know what this is?"

She thought it was a gang tattoo, but she didn't want to say so. She shook her head.

"It's okay, it's better that way. I have secrets, Abby. I could show you where the bodies are buried."

Now, her heart swelled with pity. He was bragging to her. Never mind that he was bragging about murder. He wanted to impress her, like a boy on a date with a girl too rich for him. She felt like crying, but coughed and cleared her throat instead. "Your tattoo is amazing," she managed.

He turned his leg so that she could see it in its ghoulish entirety, then let the pant leg drop and stood straight again.

"I'd like to hear your stories," she said.

"Chill, Abby." He shot a surreptitious glance in the direction of 'Lipe. "Not now. We'd have to be alone."

"Of course. You know what?" she said. "I'm getting tired. I'm an old lady compared to you guys. Would you mind if I called my friend now to come over?" She was suddenly exhausted and wanted to go home.

He considered for a moment.

"It's her car, after all."

"All right, but I'll do the talking."

"Okay."

They trooped back to the bodega. The young man pointed at the black wall phone and snapped his fingers. The counterman passed the receiver to Abby. "What the numbers?" he asked. He punched them into the dial pad. Abby had believed the phone was out of order. She almost took pride in learning that the young man's influence extended to the bodega.

Esther picked up on the first ring. "Where the hell are you?

I thought you'd be home by seven-thirty. I was ready to call the police."

Abby looked at her watch: half-past eight. It seemed to her not that the time had passed quickly, but that it had stopped altogether. "Me too. I had a little accident. With the car."

The young man grabbed the receiver from her. "Listen," he said, "your friend is okay, we had a fender-bender at the corner of North Berry and the river. She wants you to come over." Abby could hear the voice at the other end rising and falling unintelligibly, like a radio caught between stations. "Where did you find such a weirdo for a friend?" He fell silent for a moment, listening to Esther.

"Tell her to take a cab," Abby said. "The car is drivable."

"Did you hear that?" the young man asked. "And make it quick, all right?" Then he said into the phone, "Me? You can call me Chief."

He hung up and they walked back into the street, to the cars. "I wonder if your friend is going to be as crazy as you," he said.

"She's a painter, so of course she is nuts," Abby dead-panned.

He took her aside, out of 'Lipe's hearing, and scribbled on a piece of paper. "This is my pager number. I only give it to good customers, *comprendes?*"

She nodded. She realized she still didn't know his name but something prevented her from asking.

"When you call, you enter a code to page me, and then your phone number. Your code number is going to be . . . special." He smiled as it came to him. "Six-six-six for the crazy brown lady from Florida."

She gulped. She knew it was a bad number.

"It's a joke, don't look so serious," he told her. "If you call me, I'll tell you my stories." The expression on his face was eager, sincere. "Have you ever written a book?"

"No. I write articles."

"You'll have to keep my identity secret," he warned. "I don't want to end up dead." He signaled 'Lipe to rejoin them.

"You should move to Florida. You could have a good life and you wouldn't have to worry about ending up dead by the time you're thirty." She patted his hand.

"I've never even been to the beach, right, 'Lipe? I don't even know how to swim." His eyes focused behind Abby, like someone at sea searching the horizon for land. Was he about to catalogue the deprivations of his life? Would everything come pouring out, all the slights and pains and missed opportunities? It sickened her to think of him never going far from this corner, staking his whole life on this one rotten spot and the transactions that flourished there like weeds in pavement.

He touched the Puerto Rican flag hanging limply from his car antenna. "I've never even been to Puerto Rico."

"You could learn to swim. It's easy." *Come to the pool with me tonight,* she wanted to say, *and I'll teach you, and then I'll teach you how to live.*

'Lipe said, "The closest we ever been to the beach is the swimsuit issue of *Sports Illustrated.*"

They all laughed.

When Esther arrived, the young man recounted the evening's events. He shaped the story as if he and Esther were insiders and Abby an eccentric outsider. Esther kept a straight face and was polite. She was obviously frightened, which seemed to please him. "You're right," she said toward the end. "Abby is a little crazy because she lives in the suburbs. She's no New Yorker."

"Yeah. Hey, have you been to Florida?"

"Sure."

"Esther is from Florida," Abby pitched in. "We went to high school together."

"So how come she left if it's so great?"

"I'm an artist," Esther explained. "New York is the capital of the art world."

"Right," he said. He tapped the face of his wristwatch and glanced at 'Lipe. "We got to go now."

Even though she was relieved, Abby also felt a pang of regret. His departure was so abrupt, the encounter so unfinished. "Good-bye, then," she said. "And good luck."

The two men got into the Lincoln. The young man backed up and turned the vehicle around, then cruised slowly by the women, his arm extended through the window in a silent thumbs-up farewell.

The women waited until the Lincoln was out of sight. Then, wordlessly, they picked up the fender, the chrome headlight trim, and other usable pieces and climbed into the Toyota.

On the ride home, Esther accepted Abby's offer to pay for fixing the car.

Esther told Abby she was completely insane for trying to call the cops, for talking to the guy, most of all for touching him (which Abby confessed to inadvertently). "I guess he's not much of a drug dealer if he couldn't peel off a couple of hundred to cover it," Esther observed.

"He must be a small-time drug dealer."

"Maybe he's not a drug dealer at all. Maybe he's just a thug who protects the corner, you know, extorts money not to bust up the stores."

"Oh," said Abby. "Oh." The idea had never occurred to her. It was distressing to imagine that each of them might have lied to the other about the essential facts of their lives.

Something strange happened when they got back to Esther's apartment: Abby began to feel afraid. The whole evening, she told Esther, it was as if someone else had taken over her body. That other Abby was not afraid. In fact, she was optimistic beyond words, though, she conceded, possibly also naïve to hope that if she treated the young man like anyone else, he would respond in kind.

Esther poured her two shots of whiskey in quick succession, but the more Abby sipped, the more frightened she became.

Esther said, "Whatever he is, that guy could have killed you and wouldn't have thought twice."

"This is so weird," Abby said. "I've never been scared in retrospect." She was quite drunk by then.

"What were you thinking arguing with him, for God's sake?"

Abby wasn't *thinking* anything, she said, if that meant strategizing in a rational way. She'd only felt her brain engage that way twice—when she asked to get out of the car, and when she lied about being a journalist. She could not explain why she hadn't been scared out of her skin by the young man, especially since everyone else seemed to be. What but fear could have kept the onlookers away, tucked inside the small stores and apartments lining the street?

By the end of the evening, when she passed out, still terrified in her bones, Abby could offer no explanation for her behavior toward the young man that was satisfactory to her, or—in the months that followed—to anyone else. Her friends admired her empathy; her husband chided her for being a Pollyanna. For a long time she was comfortable believing that she had escaped unscathed because she was a singularly compassionate, if not saintly person.

She held on to the scrap of brown paper with his pager number, tucking it in a series of wallets. She would have called him, she told herself, if she hadn't lied about being a reporter or could figure a way out of the lie without damaging his image of her.

When she finally threw the scrap away, she felt awful, as if she had thrown away the young man himself.

She thought frequently about him after that, but without the optimism she had felt on the street and with a new sadness, the result of admitting she was helpless to change his life. Eventually, though, she became convinced that his future might take a different direction, and that it hung upon a single question: was she as unique as her friends had flattered her into thinking? If so, then the young man was doomed. But if she were less special, closer to the norm than she liked to believe, then perhaps the young man had a chance. Perhaps he would encounter others who would treat him the way Abby had, who would look at him and see simply a young man with a bright future.

The Summer of Questions

In 1966, Riva Stern was twenty years old and poised to have the best summer of her life. With the energy of a child and the freedom of an adult, she felt invincible.

At first, she'd regretted not staying in Cambridge, even if it meant living with a zillion roommates in one of the rat holes near Harvard University. After a week at home in Washington, DC, she was restless and lonely, anxious for her job at the H. G. Withers Company to begin. Mr. Withers had made his fortune by investing with her grandfather, Pop Goldring. Everyone loved a rich Jew, her grandfather said.

It was her second summer with the company and this year they had promoted her from clerk-typist to assistant bookkeeper. Pop Goldring had phoned to tell her the good news the night before she started, and to invite her to lunch at Duke Zeibert's restaurant. She loved lunch with Pop Goldring. He always bragged about her brains and her fancy college to the businessmen who joined them. He always introduced her to Duke himself. Everyone treated her like an important adult. It was a game, but she liked it nonetheless.

Riva couldn't imagine her grandfather with Mr. Withers.

Pop Goldring was talkative, with a heavy Russian accent. He wore silk suits, a Stetson, and paisley ties with matching handkerchiefs. Mr. Withers looked Edwardian by comparison, his face tucked inside a starched white collar. A plain gold stickpin pierced his tie beneath a tight Windsor knot.

On her first morning at work, she had waited ten minutes to see Mr. Withers. Finally he emerged from his office, his hand extended lancelike in front of him. They exchanged pleasantries. He looked at his watch and said he was sorry, he had an appointment. "It was so nice to see you again." And then, as an afterthought, "I guess you're glad to have your cousin here for company."

"What?"

"Your cousin, David Goldring."

"He's working here?"

"In mortgages, as a finance officer. Didn't your grandfather tell you?"

"No, he didn't." Riva's mind was racing. Her gorgeous cousin was a finance officer? A *finance* officer? That sounded yards better than assistant bookkeeper. How could that be? David was a dumb blond, a freshman at the local community college where kids who couldn't get into a good school went. David's father, Uncle Mel, was a social climber who snubbed Riva's family because his sister, Riva's mother, was married to a man who made his living as a house painter. The fact that the Goldrings were richer than the Sterns infuriated Riva. Uncle Mel was not, after all, a lawyer or a doctor. He was a builder, and wasn't that just a few notches up from house painter, prestigewise? The biting injustice of it! She might become a Communist or a Marxist. Or famous. She probably wouldn't be rich—professors rarely were—but she would be famous for something. Maybe for anthropology, like Margaret Mead.

———

Later that day, when Riva arrived at Duke Zeibert's for lunch, the first thing she saw was the interloper, cousin David, sitting among the men at her grandfather's table. She felt a rush of anger. She'd last seen David at Passover, during spring break. Uncle Mel had had a kidney stone that winter and it must have scared him, because he visited her family, a rare occurrence, though they all lived within ten minutes of each other in the northwest section. David had arrived separately in his black Thunderbird convertible. The adults had a schnapps and the kids ate ice cream. Afterward, David took Riva for a ride. The car was sleek and fast, a shiny shadow. She sat jammed in the tiny backseat behind David's sister, Polly. David kept turning around, smiling—or was it smirking?—at her. When he dropped her off, he told her to look in a mirror and promise never to comb her hair again.

Now, to her surprise, while Pop Goldring talked business with his colleagues, David focused all his attention on her. She had expected him to be a show-off; instead, he plied her with questions and listened raptly to her answers. What was she studying? How did her parents feel about her going north to college? What was her room at school like? Did she miss having boys around? He was relaxed, his coat jacket draped across his chair, one arm casually resting along the back of hers. The hairs on Riva's neck bristled when he adjusted his arm or brushed against her. Out of the corner of her eye she caught a gratified expression on Pop Goldring's face. There was no place for her anger, with her grandfather so pleased by their apparent comradeship, the food so delicious, and David so friendly. In her experience, girls usually asked the questions, while boys, armored in silence, acted as if they had no need for anything so mundane as personal information. She had never known a boy who talked so much.

The bookkeeping department, consisting of eight women, was located in the back of the building, far removed from public access, like a harem. With a slanted floor and rows of desks, it could have been one of the science lecture halls at Radcliffe. Two floor-to-ceiling windows overlooked Dumpsters in the alley below. Above, narrowing parallelograms of the neighboring high-rises soared, with slim wedges of sky between. Pigeons roosted on the ledges. To prevent the birds from crashing into the glass, the women had affixed decals, creating a zany stained-glass effect.

The Withers Company and places like it had special rules for female employees: they were forbidden to wear trousers or to smoke. Riva loved to smoke. Adding insult to injury, the women were required to keep ashtrays on their desks for visitors. When the office was crowded with men awaiting tabulations, wisps of smoke snaked between the desks like the first signs of a brush fire. Riva hated it when the men left their cigarettes smoldering under her nose.

Her first task was to balance the company's four checking accounts. She began by arranging a thousand checks in numerical order, then ran a tally of rents and expenses. Her head swam with numbers day and night. After work, house addresses and phone numbers, price tags and license plates jumped out at her, demanding to be sequenced. She took Excedrin every evening of the first week for leaden headaches.

Other than Alma, the senior bookkeeper, the women almost never left their desks or ventured into the other offices. On slow days, you might have thought they were praying, the room was so quiet, their heads bent to their adding machines at such a tender, uniform angle. Twin shafts of sunlight moved over them like a shifting benediction as the day progressed. Once, Mr. Withers came to Bookkeeping and stopped at Alma's desk, set off to the side. The two conferred in low voices. Riva looked up as Alma scraped back her chair and linked her arm inside Mr. Withers's as if they were about to dance. Instead she escorted him to the exit. Mr. Withers kept his hand on the doorknob, too polite, Riva thought, to flee, while Alma kept talking, one hand on her hip, the other gesturing fancily in the air.

Riva saw nothing of David at first and didn't know where in the building he worked. She was relieved not to be near him, not to hear herself compared to him or listen to flattery intended for Pop Goldring's ears. Then one day he appeared at her desk looking spectacularly handsome in a baby blue cord suit, his hair buzzed short except for a pale gold wave that fell forward into his eyes. He could have passed for an angel in a Renaissance painting. Nothing about him resembled the Goldrings, who had stocky peasant bodies and coarse facial features.

Riva had trouble evaluating her own looks. She knew she was not a great beauty, but boys had been asking her out since she was thirteen. Her vision of herself was limited to the static frontal view that greeted her each morning at the sink—the puzzled face of a girl inspecting her face.

David tamped a Marlboro down, lit it, and tossed the match into her ashtray. "Do you like working here?"

"It's okay. How about you?"

"I like it better than school." He pawed through a stack of papers on her desk.

"Maybe you're studying the wrong thing."

"I'm studying business, but they want you to be well-rounded, you know? So that means composition and European history and Spanish."

"You could go to Spain and rewrite their history while you sell them Hoover uprights."

David dropped his eyes, dragged on his cigarette, then exhaled the smoke with a casual sigh. "Actually I've been to Europe. We did a three-week tour when I was fifteen."

Riva hadn't meant to mouth off. It must be awful not to like school. She couldn't imagine it. "I didn't mean to be sarcastic."

"Don't worry about it."

His magnanimity made her feel worse. "I'm dying for a cigarette. We can't even smoke in the bathroom."

"Close your eyes and open your mouth."

Riva complied. He leaned toward her and exhaled.

She imagined a smoke ring settling onto her mouth. No, smoke in the shape of a kiss. Why did every conversation with David feel intimate? He'd probably become one of those business types who cut deals in swimming pools and on ski slopes, convincing everyone he knew of their uniqueness as he cadged an empire. Her eyes watered from the smoke.

"Can I give you a ride home?" He picked up a handful of paper clips and let them slip in a bright cascade through his fingers.

"You drive to work?" Riva rode the bus and liked it. She was intrigued by the other riders, especially the working girls, whose made-up faces changed from fresh and colorful in the morning, to faded and wistful in the evening. "Where do you park? I mean, it must cost your whole salary."

"They gave me a company space."

None of the women in Riva's family worked; they considered it beneath them. They had married well and would have found the bookkeepers pitiful, separated all day from their children (if they had any), exhausted by the time they returned home to a bowl of defrosting beef chuck and a lackluster husband (if they had one).

Oblivious to such pity, the bookkeepers seemed completely content with their lives and each other. Alma, the head of the department, was jolly and direct, the undisputed leader in the office and the first floor deli, where Riva joined them daily for lunch. Alma regaled them with dirty jokes, which she collected the way Riva's aunts accumulated blue willowware and gold charms for their bracelets. Over lunch, the women breezily shared recipes and diets, counted each other's calories, and related terrible stories of cancer of the breast, cervix, uterus, and bladder. Sometimes when Riva was with them, she thought she sensed food moving down her gullet, her intestines churning, sugar levels adjusting in her blood. They tasted each other's food, smoked until the last moment, then rushed to the restroom to mask the odor with breath spray and cologne. Their clothes stunned her: red button earrings and seamed stockings, though the fashion for them had passed a decade before; saucy bolero jackets accented with white summer jewelry. Each woman cultivated a different look, unlike Riva's classmates at Radcliffe who turned out for mixers in a solid phalanx of wool sheath skirts and cashmere sweaters. Perfectly applied lipstick was a high priority. The trash baskets accumulated drifts of disembodied smiles on facial tissue. Scarlet, fuchsia, coral, creamy pinks: bookkeeping was a hothouse where each woman bore a single succulent flower that was rooted deep in her body and bloomed through her mouth like a forced bulb.

One day, while Riva was counting out her share of the tip, Alma hung back to talk. "What are you studying at college?" she asked, adjusting the gold clasp of her cinch belt. Riva knew that Alma had attended secretarial "college" after high school. She'd been at the Withers Company ever since—for twenty-three years. A crack bookkeeper, the main office likened her to a man.

"Anthropology, with a minor in botany."

Alma furrowed her brow. "Do you meet men in that field?"

"Not really. Radcliffe is a girls' college."

"Well, sweetie, how are you planning on getting your M.R.S. degree? You don't want to go through life alone, do you?"

"No, but—"

"I'd have studied nursing, met myself a doctor." Alma stashed the money for the tip and the check under a plate. "I wouldn't have worked very long."

Riva had heard that Alma lived with her invalid mother, whom she now pictured as a tiny body in a sleigh bed layered in quilts.

"I'd be taking vacations in the Bahamas and Bermuda," Alma continued, "summer jaunts to Europe. Oh well."

"Where did you go for your last vacation?" Riva asked, trying to get the conversation off this track.

"I took a cruise through the Panama Canal with a friend. Couldn't be gone too long or I'd have done the Suez."

"Why the Panama Canal? I mean, it sounds nice and all."

Alma threw her jacket over one shoulder. "A man, a plan, a canal—Panama," she recited, and disappeared into the Ladies'.

On the rides home Riva and David rarely discussed anything topical. David wasn't interested in the facts and correspondences of the world, in history, biology, art, or nature. Instead, he continued to interrogate Riva about the dimmest corners of her life, every part of her body. What size dress did she wear? What size shoe? Did she suffer bad cramps? Was her family maid an ally or an enemy? (His maid hated him.) Sometimes the inquisition was eerily personal and pointless. "What are you going to do after I drop you off?" he asked, dumping the ashtray, and, "What were you thinking just now before I picked you up?" His tone was insistent and unchanging; *firmly nonchalant* was how she thought of it. And he'd answer any query she devised. "Ask me," he'd say, blandly. "Go ahead and ask me whatever you want." But few pressing questions occurred to Riva.

After David's first visit, Alma, too, besieged Riva with queries: Did David have a girlfriend? Did he play sports? Had his looks gone to his head? "Sugar," Alma explained, "I've got to keep my little black book up to date." Riva chuckled politely, but didn't answer. Alma continued to quiz her, trying to create a running gag: "What's our dreamboat up to? Has he been promoted to vice president yet?" Riva joked back, but she never let on she knew a thing about David.

That summer Riva began lying to her mother in order to spend time with David. It was surprisingly easy to pull off. Her mother trusted her: she had always been more anxious about what might happen *to* Riva than about what Riva might do of her own volition. But now she expressed little curiosity about Riva's comings and goings. In place of her usual barrage of questions, there was a distracted silence. Mrs. Stern's suspicions and worries were focused instead on Mr. Stern, who had been coming home after ten P.M. He had a government painting contract with a penalty deadline, Mrs. Stern said, and it was making his ulcers act up. The few nights he was home for supper, he was sullen and abrasive. Neither Riva nor her mother spoke at the table, for fear of setting him off.

Riva did, however, tell the truth about spending the Fourth of July weekend with David and his family at Rehoboth Beach. Mrs. Stern was flattered that Uncle Mel and Aunt Avery had invited Riva, as if royalty had deigned to socialize with a commoner. Riva did not tell her that David had suggested the idea to his parents or that she and David were driving up in a separate car, though Mrs. Stern probably would not have objected. Any attention from the Goldrings was desirable.

He picked her up at nine on Saturday morning. With the top down, it was impossible to talk. They listened to the radio for the two-hour trip to Delaware. David wore a safari hat and smoked furiously, his cigarettes red coals in the wind. Riva felt nervous. The ride was long and for the first time she couldn't pretend they were together because they were cousins or because they worked at the same office. What if it was love? Once, she had seen a short subject at the drive-in called *Only in Sweden,* about a brother and sister. The film was grainy and jerky, like a home movie, and consisted of a couple hiding their faces as they skulked through doorways. Would it be incest with David? Sometimes when first cousins married they produced hemophiliacs, like the Romanoffs. Riva felt fiendish thinking such thoughts. Probably David was just being friendly, cousinly, toward her. Probably just that.

Saturday passed rapidly, occupied with swimming, badminton, and strolling on the beach. The house was full of people. David's sister, Polly, had brought a friend. His parents had invited a couple with a baby and spent much of their time fussing over the infant. After dark, they launched fireworks and watched them slick the ocean with color. Riva slept downstairs in the den. She heard Polly and her friend giggling at one A.M., then the house grew quiet until the only sound was surf rummaging over shingle, like someone returning to a troublesome idea again and again.

On Sunday, David was moody and distant. He surf-fished all morning, leaving Riva to clean up a messy breakfast of omelets and hotcakes. Polly and her friend occupied the den, banging on the player piano. Riva lay on the beach until it was time to leave. Other than polite remarks ("How's your mother, Riva dear?"), Mel and Avery hadn't spoken with her, and she was too shy to initiate a conversation. She and David hadn't exchanged more than a greeting all day.

She thanked Mel and Avery. David tossed everything into the trunk and spun out of the driveway, spraying gravel. Ten minutes later, he turned onto a two-lane road Riva didn't recognize. "Where are you going?"

"I'm taking the long way back. The scenery is better."

Riva watched the lush roadside slip past. Virginia creeper and foxgrape spanned the culverts like green trampolines. They passed fields of tobacco, watermelon, and corn. The gas stations and tackle stores were quaint, with wooden screen doors and squat gas pumps. David pointed to a frozen custard shop with a giant sugar cone on the roof of the drive-through. "Want some?" he asked. Riva demurred.

He bought a double scoop of chocolate, and parked the

car in the shade of a mulberry tree, lapping steadily at the custard.

"I've changed my mind," Riva said. "Could I have a taste?"

He extended the custard to her. Riva took a lick of the sweet concoction. David leaned forward and began licking until he touched her tongue with his cold and tremulous one. They kissed for a long time. "I've been wanting to do that forever," David whispered.

"You hardly spoke to me today. You were downright rude."

"I know it. Sorry. Extreme horniness." He kissed her again, his tongue twisting and turning in her mouth, sending pleasure everywhere.

"I can't believe we're doing this." She felt a surge of pride, the pride of conquest. *Family knockout falls for family brain. Family shocked!*

"You know," David said, "my father and I watched you on *Youth Wants to Know* every Sunday. You were terrific. You made Senator Thurmond look like an ass."

This pleased Riva as much as the kissing. The TV show, on which smart high school students grilled public figures, had made her feel like a celebrity. "Our family would be horrified to see us together." Riva briefly pictured Pop Goldring's face, the veins standing out in furor.

"I know." He leaned back and squinted at the sun. "Don't you feel weird?"

"Yes," she admitted. "After all, I'm a year older than you."

"That's not what I mean. It's like our families would disapprove not just because we're related, but because they don't get along." David lay down in her lap and pulled her face to his. "It would be jealousy. Sheer jealousy."

When Riva got home that Sunday evening, her father dozed in his blue velvet easy chair, his feet on a hassock, a copy of *Field and Stream* splayed open on the floor.

The TV was on, but her mother wasn't watching it. She sat in the dining room, blowing her nose and running her fingers through her short, thick hair. The silver chest, its lid gaping, trays and slots emptied, had been moved from the buffet to the table. Silver flatware was mounded up in the center of the table. Usually the maid polished the silver. Why was it dumped out like pick-up sticks on a Sunday night? "Is everything all right?" Riva asked.

Her mother tucked her handkerchief back into her bosom. "My allergies are acting up, that's all."

"Why's the silver out?"

"It's too late for questions. Go to bed, dear. You have to work tomorrow."

They decided that eating lunch together at work would arouse suspicion. Cousins wouldn't be so chummy.

Except for David, Riva's world that year consisted of women—her classmates at Radcliffe during the school months, her mother, and the steadfast bookkeepers with their nylon stockings rasping in the summer. She admired her coworkers for their self-sufficiency and at the same time feared her life might turn out like theirs. Look what happened if you held out too long—Alma, clad in tight skirts and tucked-in sweaters. She had a pretty face framed by short, dyed, reddish-brown hair brushed back over her ears into a duck's ass. Bangs fell on her forehead in jaunty points. But up close, the picture altered: flecks of food between her long teeth; lipstick bleeding into the puckers around her mouth; pitiful worn-out blouses and skirts; outmoded stilettos. And hopeless flirtations with the Withers men, a hand fluttering at her hair or throat, her voice dropping to a husky register, then curling to a kittenish pitch.

Uncle Mel and Aunt Avery had tickets for *Madame Butterfly* at the Carter Barron amphitheater and decided not to go. David told them it was the kind of thing Riva would like, and offered to escort her.

"Keep convincing them I'm a good influence on you and maybe they'll invite me and my family for dinner sometime," Riva said in the car that night.

"We never invite anybody to the house for dinner. We take them to restaurants. It's tax deductible that way," David said.

"Never? Not even once in a while?"

David eased into the traffic funneling through the hilly entrance to the theater. "Only my rich Mexican godparents who stay the weekend."

"Anyway," Riva pointed out, "with your family it isn't deductible."

"It's not about taxes," David said. "Our families just don't get along."

"But *I've* never done anything to them. I, Riva, am innocent as the driven—"

"Let's change the subject, okay? I haven't done anything to you, either. I'm sure they have their reasons on both sides."

She slid across the seat and put her hand to his cheek. The skin was baby-bum soft above the razor line. "You're right," she whispered. She slid back to her side of the car. They had to be careful. The sun wasn't down yet and somebody they knew might spot them.

Neither of them could concentrate on the show. A silky evening wind lifted their hair and traced curlicues on their bare legs and arms, as if to remind them of the glories of touch. They rose from their seats for intermission. David said, "I've had enough. Meet me at the car, J-11." He trotted away into the darkness. "I've got a surprise."

When Riva reached the parking lot, she spied the green of his shirt in an oak tree, illuminated by a distant parking lot light. His arm moved, a sliver of moon rocking in the blue-black air. "David, what are you doing?"

"Come up here, Riva."

Feeling her way, she climbed onto a picnic bench under the oak. He helped her to a platform nailed between two big branches where he was perched. Her shoes dropped off. She bounced on the platform, testing it. "Do you think this is solid? David, what are you doing?"

He'd lifted her pink cotton skirt and was kissing the inside of her thigh. She leaned back, wedged herself in the rough crook of the tree and lay still as David plied her with his tongue and fingers. The tree bark dug into her back and neck, sharpening the sensations. When they kissed, she could smell herself on his mouth. She licked his lips, dizzy on the taste. In the distance, Madame Butterfly pined for her foreign soldier as David teased her to two orgasms.

He helped her down onto the picnic table at the tree's shrouded base, then got on top of her. It turned out he was an athlete; he could do it for a long time and not finish and not get tired. She was so moved by his performance that back in the car, convinced she was in love, she took him in her hand until he scattered like a milkweed.

━━

"I know you don't want me to bring this up, but I want to know why your parents don't like me and my family," Riva said. They were on their way home from work on a sticky day at the end of July. David had just pulled into the parking lot of Riva's apartment building. Instead of following the circular drive, he headed for the farthest corner and parked.

"They do like you. A whole lot. They admire you."

"Why do I feel so strange when I'm around them?"

"I don't know. Anyway, take it from me, you wouldn't want to spend time with them. They're horrible snobs. Besides, Uncle Harry hasn't invited your family over for dinner, either, right? What's the difference?"

It was true. Neither of her mother's brothers or their wives socialized with the Sterns. "The difference is that I don't care about Uncle Harry and Aunt Florence. They're sickening and their kids are sickening."

David laughed. "Still, it's all the same thing."

"What do you mean?"

"I mean, I guess the reason is the same."

"What reason?"

David swatted at a mosquito that wobbled slowly through his open window. "I was just thinking of, well, you know, the big rift."

Riva pictured big rocks with edges sharp enough to butcher meat, a deep blue chasm between them. "The what?"

"You know, the big falling out years ago." David put his arms around her and rubbed her neck.

She sat up very still and straight. "What falling out?"

"You really don't know?" He groaned and dropped his hands into his lap. "I feel completely rotten now."

Riva felt hollow. "How come you know and I don't and it's about *my* family?"

"It never occurred to me you didn't know," David mumbled.

"Just tell me, okay?" Riva demanded. "I want you to tell me right now."

"Okay. Probably everyone in Washington knows that your father took the payroll check from Goldring Brothers and blew it at the track. I think there were things before that, but that was the straw that broke the camel's back."

Riva knew that her father had once worked for the Goldrings, overseeing construction jobs, sometimes painting and wallpapering.

"Everybody knows he's got a problem. You know, the gambling."

Her father a gambler? He'd stolen Uncle Mel's payroll? That made him a criminal. The air in her lungs felt like ice.

All at once she knew it had to be true. Once, as a little girl, she'd mistaken the reflections on a lake for real houses and trees until something disturbed the surface and they shattered into incoherent ripples. Now the image of her family fractured into flimsy splotches and dashes of color separated by an impenetrable blackness. She recalled her father telling her about an acquaintance who'd wager on anything. "Even which raindrop would hit the sill first," he'd said, disapprovingly. He must have been describing himself.

"I'm sorry. I wish I hadn't brought it up. I thought you knew."

"I'm going in now." Before David could say anything else, Riva climbed out and closed the door. "I'm fine," she told him. She waited until his car was out of sight before entering her apartment building.

She felt as if she had failed the most fundamental of tests, like that eighth grade geography quiz where she couldn't distinguish the square western states from one another and received a humiliating F. House painting was not the problem. Uncle Mel was not the problem. Officially it was ulcers that had ruined her father's life. Did he even have ulcers? Or had the stolen payroll eaten a hole in his gut? Her mother never spoke of anything substantial, no matter what disasters were brewing. This, Riva had always supposed, was to shelter her from life's difficulties. Now, she realized, it was her mother's way of protecting herself. Either way, Riva was left feeling inept at coping. Not to mention being the last person on Earth to know her father had a gambling problem.

Riva remembered the silver flatware mounded up on the table, all the times her mother's eyes had appeared too red. Always allergies. A cold. Never, *Yes, Riva, your father is a bum, a criminal, a louse. He stole the family payroll. He hocked my wedding rings, the candlesticks, my beaver coat.*

She peered into her parents' bedroom: a suite of dark, polished mahogany furniture, the pair of prints above the headboard—"Blue Boy" and "Blue Girl" padding through a wooded glen. Pathetic attempts to add the patina of decency to their union. What furtive bargain had her parents struck? Until now, they had both seemed ordinary and predictable. Where did her father go every night if he wasn't painting government buildings?

Her mother was setting the dining table with the good flatware again, perhaps to count it, Riva thought. More camouflage, the covering over of unpleasant realities with glittery surfaces. All her mother's energy had been diverted into flourishes and frills. The chandelier cast a silver cap over Mrs. Stern's short, dyed black hair. "How long have you been home?" she asked Riva. "I didn't hear you come in."

———

Alma stopped asking about David, as if he had dropped off the planet. And then one morning at work, Riva saw something from the periphery of her eye. A lingering between Alma and David, a blurring where there should have been a crisp gesture of greeting or farewell. Though she didn't know what she had glimpsed, she believed it was significant. She replayed the scene in her mind, attempting to freeze-frame the odd movement, to convince herself it was nothing, but a faint suspicion remained, like a retinal afterimage. That night she suggested to David that they catch a movie, but he said he was busy with family stuff, his godparents visiting from Mexico. He'd be occupied for the rest of the week.

They talked on the phone instead that week, usually right before going to bed. David felt bad that he had been the one to reveal her family shame. She felt sorry for him, and loved him a little more because he could hurt for her. Reassuring him didn't seem to help. "It's not your fault," she told him. "You did me a favor telling me, it was just a painful favor. But the truth always—"

"Please, spare me your homonyms."

"Homilies."

"Yeah."

"Uh, David, there's something else I have to tell you about my family." She wanted to mention the silverware, find out what he thought.

"I'd rather not talk about that stuff again."

"Okay, well," she stumbled, "anyway, I have to take a shower." She hung up, deflated, wincing at his malapropism.

A few days later, their rides home from work stopped. David's car was on the fritz, and the part wouldn't arrive for weeks. He'd be taking the bus, too, but they lived on different routes. They spent fewer and fewer evenings together as August boiled the summer down to a sticky sludge. Though

David remained sexually attentive when they did manage a reunion, by the end of the month, he was no longer a constant feature of Riva's life. It finally dawned on her that she had been quietly dumped.

During the last week of work, Riva and Alma were chatting in the ladies' room as they took turns smoking in the stalls and standing guard. "Are you and David cooled down then? I know he was a pretty hot number with you for a while."

"Really?" Riva felt uncomfortable, exposed. This was no game. She decided not to ask how Alma came by her information.

"It was all over your face, sweetie. You smelled like David some days, if you know what I mean."

Riva dropped her cigarette into the toilet. She felt her face blanch.

"He's not quite right for you, anyway," Alma pronounced, patting her hair. "You deserve someone with more brain power."

"Why do you say that?" Riva fired back, not knowing where Alma was going with her judgment.

"Leave him to the grateful ones."

"The *grateful* ones? Who are they?"

The two women stepped into the elevator together. "Little girls maybe. He probably hangs out at the mall when he can. And older women. You can never tell with a guy like David. He keeps everything in motion. You blink, and he's somewhere else."

The doors opened and Riva strode to her desk while Alma paused at the water cooler, chatting up a man from Loans.

On the last Friday night of August, she borrowed her father's pickup truck and waited a block from David's house. At seven forty-five he vaulted into the Thunderbird. She followed him, slowly at first, her heart beating wildly. If he saw her she would die of embarrassment—sneaking after a boy in her father's car, like a scorned lover. She hung back, worried she might lose him in the dense shoal of cars on Georgia Avenue. He turned into the park; she zoomed closer. In the gathering dark it was harder to see his black car. She followed the taillights blindly along curving park roads and out again into the slower grid of the city. He turned onto Kennedy Street, made the first left and nipped into a parking space. There was no guesswork about where he was going, as if he'd been there many times. She circled the block and parked a few houses behind him, just in time to see Alma greet him with a kiss as he stood in the glow of a yellow bug light on the front porch of number 878. He followed her inside.

Back home, Riva's imagination ran wild. Alma would have given her mother a sedative, closed the windows, and turned on the AC. She and David probably talked dirty while they ate food off each other. She had never eaten dinner off anyone's belly or buttocks but she had read D. H. Lawrence and Lawrence Durrell. Or perhaps Alma liked to inflict pain. (She had read Freud, too.) She pictured Alma standing over David, twisting the heel of her pump into the sweet flesh of his neck.

At three A.M. he'd leave, kissing the now-rumpled Alma good-bye, pressing his cheek against her crusty lashes, her skin jaundiced in the porch light.

All those questions! All his intimate probing was intended to suggest that he found her fascinating. But what about her answers? The truth stabbed at her: her answers meant nothing to him. Probably with Alma his nibbling interrogations ceased. Probably Alma was the answer to all his questions.

—

On her last day of work, all the bookkeepers but Alma (who claimed to have a doctor's appointment) treated her to lunch. Afterward, they presented her with a pair of elbow-length black kid gloves from Garfinkle's, the priciest department store in town. The last signature on the card was Alma's. Underneath she had written *Find yourself a nice guy and settle down.* The women kissed her farewell, their red lip-prints rising in flocks on her cheeks. Riva knew she would likely never see them again.

In all likelihood she would not see David again for a long time. She fantasized a last conversation, and her own monologue (righteous? clever? ironic? tragic?) within it. She would phone. That way he couldn't watch her face and she could concentrate on her tone of voice, delivering just the right blow to his ego in a line he'd never forget.

"Who is it?" His voice sleepy at seven-thirty on a Saturday morning. "Riva? Is that you?" he asked, clawing his way toward consciousness.

"It's your lover, lover," she whispered.

"Riva? Is something wrong? It's so early."

"Had a late night screwing Alma?"

No, that sounded too jealous. She needed to humiliate him for the way he had dropped her—without courtesy or courage. He had been dishonorable, dishonest. "I think you're a skunk," she practiced. "A gutless wonder." No, not piercing, not clever enough.

When the time came to return to New England and school, she simply phoned to say good-bye, entrusting to the pressure of spontaneity what her intellect had failed to produce. "I hope you have a good year, a good life," she told him.

"God, you make it sound like we're never going to see each other again."

"I know. I *know,*" she said, her voice heavy with meaning. "But you don't believe that, do you? Never mind, don't answer that."

She saw Alma one more time, in Woolworth's, during Christmas break two years later. Alma was seated at the lunch counter. Her legs were tightly crossed and she was swiveling on her stool like a lure on a line, a lace strap peeking from one sleeve like the deckled edge of an invitation. She recognized Riva immediately and offered her a cigarette. They lit up, inhaling wordlessly together.

"Hey!" an old man two seats away objected. "Put those things out." The Surgeon General's report had been released recently and NO SMOKING signs had sprouted everywhere, including Woolworth's. "Can't you read?" he boomed.

Alma took another drag and stubbed the cigarette out on the floor. "You know what they say," she told Riva, loud enough for the man to overhear. "When you're not being beautiful, make trouble."

Riva laughed. Later, she would take out her pen, as she imagined Margaret Mead might, and write that one down.

Laws of Nature

Life can only be understood backward.
—KIERKEGAARD

Clad in a gold pectoral, like a Viking princess, she floated downriver seated atop a mammoth swan with feathers the size of sea oat plumes. Reins of scarlet ribbons rested lightly in one hand; she lifted the other. Someone was going to kiss it. Or was the kiss to be deposited on her emerald ring?

A loud noise startled Helen, a trumpet blown as her regal boat passed. No, a car alarm, shattering her dream of stateliness. Saturday morning. She had intended to sleep late.

Claude's side of the bed held an imprint of his body. She turned into it and inhaled his scent. He was an early riser, even on weekends. No doubt he was already daydreaming in the aisles of the Home Depot or tackling the exercise stations on the *vita* path at the park.

She slogged into the bathroom, did her business, and showered. In five minutes she was at the starting line, the mirror above the sink. She flossed her teeth, grimacing as she see-sawed the thread in every cranny. An activity that should never be done in pairs, flossing.

She stared at her reflection. Something was different, but what? She felt the same uneasiness as when she stood before the three-way mirror at Dillard's and unfamiliar views emerged—a strange hunched shoulder, thick waistline, shapely calf. . . .

She must have slept well.

She looked away, then looked back. She must have slept for a year. She had never looked so rested.

———

That afternoon, she was at Cloth World buying supplies to make a vampire costume for her grandson, Evan: black taffeta, red satin, wire, interfacing. The familiar, cranky saleswoman lined up the bolts of fabric. Helen acknowledged her with a nod. "How much would you need, then?" the woman asked.

Helen had scribbled her numbers on a scrap of paper. "Four yards of the black, one and a half of the red."

The saleswoman flipped the first bolt over several times, measured the cloth, and cut it, wincing audibly as she squeezed the scissors. "Carpal tunnel," she explained to no one in particular.

"My sister had that for years," Helen said. What could she say that would be hopeful? Dammit, now she might have to invent something. Why couldn't she keep her nose out of other people's problems?

"You resemble one of my regular customers," the saleswoman said. "Maybe it's your sister."

"No, she lives in Denver."

"Never shops at the Cloth World in Fort Myers?"

"I don't think so."

The saleswoman straightened up and punched in the

numbers on the cash register. She took Helen's credit card. "Oh," she said, jumping back a little. "You're her."

"Who?"

"My regular customer."

"Of course I am."

Flustered, the woman shook her head as if to loosen up the appropriate words. "Well, you look . . . different today. That's why I thought you were the sister."

"Must be my hair," said Helen. That's when she realized what she had seen in the mirror that morning: she looked younger.

———

That whole week she ambushed herself in mirrors: in the plate glass of store windows, the rearview of the car, even the distorting convexities of glossy automobile fenders. Reflective surfaces, she noticed, surrounded her. She had simply fallen out of the habit of acknowledging her twin in their lustrous depths. Now, she couldn't escape them, or herself.

Was the improvement she saw the result of something she was eating? The cumulative effect of the vitamins she'd been downing for years? Perhaps they had reached a critical mass, all the antioxidants finally in league to fight off the rowdy free radicals. She pictured a social revolution, like the sixties, in her bloodstream and at the portal to every organ. They were burning American fats instead of flags in protest, they were making bonfires of oversized bras. Every cell in her body was demanding freedom—the freedom of feeling better and looking younger.

Helen and Claude had planned for weeks to dine together. Claude had become so busy in the last five years that he had to schedule appointments to see his family. But success had made him happy and generous, for which Helen was grateful.

Glenda, Claude's secretary of thirty years, phoned on Friday afternoon to remind Helen of the time and place. At Claude's instruction, she had reserved a table at Chica's, a swank waterfront bistro frequented by prominent business-people. Claude was beginning to be recognized in such places. Men would walk over to pump his arm or rest a friendly hand on his shoulder like a brief, fleshy epaulet.

"You look lovely," Claude said, staring at her across the table.

"Thank you." Helen felt unaccountably content. They had a nice table overlooking the bay, the lights of Cape Coral twinkling like festive decorations on the far shore.

"New makeup?" he ventured.

"No."

"Then it must be the diet."

A waiter deposited red leatherette menus with gold tassels on the table. Then, bowing slightly, he poured water into Helen's glass from a sweating silver pitcher.

"I'm not on a diet. Do I look fat to you?" Maybe that was it. Maybe she'd put on a few pounds and the extra weight had ironed out some of her wrinkles.

"No, you don't look fat. You just look better."

They had ordered a bottle of wine, which the waiter was

stylishly decanting. She decided not to tell Claude about the other compliments of the last week and what she thought she saw in the mirror each morning after he left for work.

Claude leaned back in his chair, savoring the wine. "I've hired a new attorney."

"Congratulations. How many does that make now, seven?"

Fort Myers was the center of the biggest real estate boom in the history of the state. Claude's law practice had ballooned in the past decade. Instead of single-family home sales, he was now working and investing with land developers.

"Eight, actually. This one is bilingual. And quite beautiful."

"A good attorney, I hope."

"This is her first job out of the chute. She's raring to go."

"Great," Helen said.

A party boat strung with pastel lights and filled with dancing couples drifted by, its music just audible through the restaurant's glass walls.

Claude was scanning the patrons for a schmooze opportunity. Or maybe he was daydreaming. Now that their son was grown and settled, they didn't talk as much as they used to. After forty years of marriage, silence had become their ally. It had spared them pointless discussions when the ardor went out of their marriage for no particular reason. In the absence of a sex life, a subtle new language of touch had developed between them—entwining limbs, pats, and kisses like footnotes to a long life of bodily passion. They no longer fought. Claude said it was because of menopause. Years before he had argued that PMS was the single biggest obstacle to harmony between men and women. It had infuriated Helen at the time, but now that she had reached the placid waters of early old age, she was inclined to agree with him. They were both delighted with their lives, which had become more separate, and in some ways, more exciting. Helen had retired after thirty-eight years of high school teaching and was earning a doctorate in anthropology at Gulf Coast University. She was in no hurry, though sometimes she recoiled imagining her graduation picture in the local newspaper: a shrunken ninety-year-old in a billow of black receiving her scroll.

The waiter returned to take their orders. Helen held the menu at arm's length, adjusting her glasses up and down. Everything was fuzzy. As she removed her glasses for cleaning and dipped her napkin in ice water, the fine, looping cursive of the menu swam into view: *Demi-Raque of Baby Lamb en Croute.* "Look at that!" She touched the offending phrase on Claude's menu. "*Raque?* 'Raque' is not a word in any language! God I hate fake French. The English is pretty stinky, too. 'Baby lamb'?"

"Does it matter?" Claude looked at her in a kindly but exasperating way that suggested he knew the relative importance of things and she didn't. Now that he was making a lot of money, Claude didn't have to worry about small stuff. Only last week he had told her admiringly about a client who had cut down a mangrove tree to make room for a dock, knowing he'd incur a $10,000 fine. She hoped that success would never render Claude that arrogant and smug.

"You wouldn't be saying that if this menu were a contract," she countered.

"But it's just a menu."

"What a misguided notion of elegance. If that was on a student paper, I'd give it an F," she declared.

Claude surveyed the room. Was he even listening?

Demi-Raque of Baby Lamb en Croute. She snickered to herself at the image of a lamb kicking its way out of a pastry shell as big as a burlap sack. Then, all at once, the lamb, the pastry, the menu vanished from her thoughts. She realized that she had been reading without her glasses.

The next morning, Saturday, something else was different in the mirror: below the dyed brown hair her roots were growing in dark instead of gray.

Helen finished sewing Evan's costume, a voluminous black taffeta cape with a red satin standup collar and trim. The day before, she had bought a fabulous Dracula kit at Walgreens: wax fangs, a compact of greenish-gray makeup befitting someone who slept in a coffin, and a small tube of greasy red body paint to simulate "the Count's elixir of eternal life, the blood of the living." It was all packaged inside a spectacular container for trick-or-treat candy, a plastic bucket in the shape of a vampire head that promised to glow in the dark if illuminated for six hours beforehand. Someone had paid attention to the design: the bail was a wavy tress that matched the hair embossed on the sides of the bucket when folded flat. Evan took after Helen, he noticed details. He'd love it.

Halloween fell on a Friday and her son, Gregory, his wife,

Susan, and the kids were flying in from Seattle for the weekend. Evan was nine and Little Helen was three. Helen was flattered to have a namesake. It also gave her the willies. It reminded her of *Invasion of the Body Snatchers,* in which people discovered identical versions of themselves growing in giant bean pods. The faces of the aliens were blank, devoid of laugh and worry lines, scars, sun spots—all the evidence of a lived life. One by one, the humans died in their sleep as their pod counterparts woke up. Little Helen was an innocent toddler, but there was something creepy to Big Helen about already having her replacement on the scene.

She set the plastic head on the bathroom counter under track lighting to charge its phosphorescent cells, and imagined it hanging, a ghoulish yellow-green, from Evan's small arm as he made his rounds in the inky dark of the Palm Acres subdivision. Then she steamed the cape and hung it in the guest room closet.

She consulted her watch and hurried to her bedroom to change into her Hawaiian costume: green cellophane hula skirt, black wig, tank top, and a magic wand in keeping with the general ambiance of the holiday. She drove to the airport. Claude was in the Everglades, in Flamingo, talking to developers. She had decided to start a new tradition: when Grandpa can't go to the airport with her, Grandma meets the plane *en croute*.

In October, the air was still heavy and humid as wet blankets. With tourist season two months away, the roads were empty. In another decade, Helen feared, the roads would be clogged year-round. The entire nation, it seemed, was moving to the Florida Gulf Coast for its perpetual sunshine and mild winters. The Oaks, Gumbo Limbo, Sabal Palms: she drove past new housing sprouting like mushrooms on the roadside, each ironically named for the natural features it had supplanted. Did the residents of The Oaks realize or care that all the trees had been removed? Helen understood that it was difficult to block "progress" when money was involved, but every week as she motored past yet another newly cleared field, she sank a little deeper into her seat. She never talked to Claude about his business dealings. He knew her feelings on the subject of development.

The flight from Seattle had arrived early, and hundreds of passengers were already filing into the cramped baggage claim area. Her cellophane skirt rustling like a salt shaker, Helen plunged into the crowd. A moment later, Gregory, his wife, and the two children streamed by her. She tried to tap her son on the shoulder with her magic wand, but he was moving quickly, and she missed.

"Gregory!" she hollered. "Over here!"

"Mom?" Gregory stood about fifteen feet away trying to locate the source of her voice.

"Grandma!" Evan shrieked with delight. He rushed over and clasped her legs through the hula skirt, like someone disappearing behind a beaded curtain.

"Mom?" Gregory repeated.

━━

Her daughter-in-law, Susan, had been raised a Catholic and was now an atheist; Gregory had switched from his parents'

Unitarianism to Buddhism. The only holidays they observed with the children were Thanksgiving, Halloween, and a secular version of Christmas. Halloween was the principle one, part of a global trend, Gregory informed Helen as he set the table later that evening. Even Turks and Israelis had adopted the holiday. Everyone loved to dress up, he said, it was as simple as that.

"It's all marketing," added Claude, who had arrived just in time for dinner. "Candy and greeting card companies. And the costume manufacturers."

"Don't forget the pumpkin farmers," Gregory pitched in.

In the kitchen, Susan fussed over Helen, beginning with her cellophane skirt, but quickly turning to her appearance. "Who has a secret?" she teased gleefully as they settled the food on the table for dinner. "Come on, Big Helen, do you want to confess anything?" The others pricked up their ears.

Helen was dumbfounded. She felt guilty, though for what she had no idea.

"All right, I've got to ask," Susan said. "You had a face-lift, didn't you?"

"No!" Helen's voice boomed. How could Susan think that Helen would resort to something so . . . shallow?

"Eye job, then."

"Nothing."

Silence dropped like a veil over the entire table.

"You do look great, Big Helen," Claude affirmed. "Doesn't she?"

There was a clamoring of agreement.

"But I can vouch for it." Claude touched Helen's cheek. "No surgery for Big Helen."

"Big Helen" did not fit her any more than the idea of a face-lift. It belonged to a Greek woman with a hooked nose and barrel chest, golden sandals, a bronze shield like Achilles. How had she relinquished her name?

The compliments flowed in a torrent throughout the visit. Gregory and Susan said she looked young, energetic, and even "dazzling." Helen couldn't help but deduce what lurked behind all this flattery, namely, how she had appeared to them before: old, lethargic, and even dull. It was praise founded on insult, and her feelings ran the gamut from joy to anger, pride to outrage. Had she looked so terrible before? What louts! Had they even noticed her before or wondered about her existence before they entered her life? Apparently no one but Claude understood that she had once been an attractive young woman.

Everyone claimed to be happy for her, but privately, Helen believed they were appalled. All but Benita, the housekeeper, who was completely unperturbed by Helen's changes. Benita had worked for Helen for more than twenty years and Helen had watched her grow from a timid girl to a matronly señora.

The Monday after the children left, Benita came to help put the house back in order. "The Missus is changing, looking younger," she noticed matter-of-factly as the two women pinned blankets to air on the clothesline.

"You don't seem surprised," Helen said.

Benita told her that in her native village in Mexico, older

women frequently underwent radical changes. Occasionally they showed up as other people, usually their own ancestors. But more often they changed into pigs or wolves. It happened all the time.

Though as an anthropologist Helen was familiar with animal totems and spirit guides, she was certain she didn't quite grasp what Benita was saying. Surely there was a degree of metaphor involved. Surely the wolf- and pig-women didn't stalk small animals or forage for garbage, then hurry home to cook dinner. "Do they ever turn back into human beings?" she asked.

"Not usually." Benita began hosing off the patio furniture. "Their children are grown, their husbands, they have girlfriends. Nobody wants them. They roam the countryside together in packs."

Helen visualized shaggy wolves huddled in the moonlight, their throats raised skyward in ghostly howls. But pigs? All she could summon were pink piglets nosing the teats of a sow. "Bands of pigs run wild in the countryside?"

"*Sí*, pigs run together, too. Wild ones, with the big teeth."

Helen scrapped the barnyard image for wild hogs and peccaries charging through the woods.

"Sometimes the pigs like to set fire to things."

"How? I mean, if they're pigs they have no hands." Helen opened the back door and they went inside.

Benita rolled her eyes and sighed, as if the answer were self-evident. "They are magical pigs, *claro*. They have the power of the mind."

"Of course." When Helen thought about it later, it seemed plausible.

———

Several years before, when Helen turned sixty, she had become, for all intents and purposes, invisible, except for isolated body parts at doctors' and dentists' offices. So invisible that only last semester a student in the cafeteria had dumped his dirty dishes at her table while she was eating lunch. "Excuse me?" she had protested, indignant. "You're excused," he had replied, smirking. Her very presence was negligible. Socially speaking, she no longer counted, like being naked in front of a dog. Her status had plummeted to such a degree, she figured, that had she been a chimpanzee, there wouldn't have been an animal low enough in rank to groom her; she would be hungry, dirty, mad with biting fleas. Had she been an Eskimo, she'd have been put out on the ice by now, left to freeze and then defrost the following spring, a puddle of putrid flesh. Claude and Greg, clad in bearskins, might trek through her damp remains and simply wipe their feet clean in the snow.

Often in grad school classes, her comments went unremarked, as if she were inaudible or her voice had bewitched her classmates into a trance from which they would awaken, lively and enthusiastic moments later when someone else, usually a man, repeated her idea.

Nevertheless, she enjoyed school. Whether she was teaching or listening, the classroom always gave her a solid sense of purpose. It was a good thing, for if she had followed the traditional role, aging into a family matriarch, her functions would have been scant and titular indeed. She would have reigned over one child, one child-in-law, and two grandchildren, all of whom lived across the country, none of whom had a spare ten minutes in a day. They were hardly a clan big enough to be concerned about primogeniture or currying the favor of queen mothers.

As the crone in Helen vanished, her hair grew in as shiny and pliable as new leaves. Some days, springing from bed to greet herself in the mirror, tears flowed freely. She had missed the old Helen, that is, her younger self. The cheer and optimism she had always carried in her heart were once again bodily present in the firmness of her lip line, the clarity of her gaze, her nimble gait, and upright posture. Once again, she looked determined, not defeated.

Was it possible she was actually *becoming* younger, organically, the same way all her life she had relentlessly aged?

Her family doctor agreed that she looked fifteen years younger since her last visit, but her blood work was normal and he could offer no explanation. His demeanor was lugubrious, as if he had just diagnosed a fatal disease. He wrote the name of a psychiatrist on a pad, tore it off, and passed it to her. "Even if it's temporary," he said, "you'll have to learn to cope with it."

Outside, she threw the paper away. Cope? How about *celebrate*? She wasn't going to worry about adjusting. She was tired of having a handle on everything. She felt like sprinting down the beach, splashing the onlookers at the community pool with a cannonball from the diving board.

She took up tennis again, gently, then with more vigor and verve as she realized that her knees, once sere and creaky beneath their hood of bone, were juicy as peaches.

Her back and belly fat melted away, leaving an alluring figure, a waist not seen in more than a decade. She now looked younger than her sister, ten years her junior. She began to menstruate again. Benita kept telling her how pretty she looked. She suggested Helen wear brighter colors—red, especially, because her fire had returned.

Claude, however, was appalled when he spied pads wrapped up in the bathroom wastebasket one morning in late February. His face turned ashen. "This is terrible," he said, rushing from the room. He left for work right after. But by that evening, he was contrite. "I'm sorry I upset you," he said, putting his arm around her.

This was what Helen thought of as his generic apology, evolved over decades because he knew it was expected and that nothing else worked as well to restore peace. This time, though, his apology saddened her. She wanted to reassure him that she felt as robust and even-keeled as the granddaddy oak in the backyard. She was sure she wasn't having PMS. "I don't think I'm having PMS," she said.

"That's the problem. You never thought you were having PMS. That's what's so damn insidious about it. It's convincing, like mental illness."

"But this time really is different—"

"That's exactly what you used to say."

"I did?" She couldn't recall.

"Yes. You'd take vitamin E or eat lima beans and then you thought you weren't having it. But you were."

"Maybe so," Helen conceded. "Let's just wait and see."

"All right," Claude said.

They cuddled for a long time in bed that evening before dropping off to sleep. The next morning, Helen moved the wastebasket under the sink, out of view, so as not to announce her cycle on the off chance she was wrong.

———

At the student union, Helen spent her lunches observing her younger classmates. She wanted to tell them how delectable they were, but she knew that despite their perfect hair and nails and physiques and muscle tone and teeth, none of them would believe her. When she was young, she and her friends, male and female, had been likewise hypercritical of themselves and each other, adhering to an unattainable standard of beauty that was near-pathological. All this insecurity did was prevent orgies, she realized now. The energy that could have fueled their desire was spent instead feeding uncertainty. The modern world had replaced tribal taboos with the pangs of inferiority, dogma with personal insecurity and unhappiness. Now individuals suffered in the name of social order and didn't even know it. She remembered her grandmother exclaiming over the beauty of each grandchild. What she had thought was the vanity of a doddering old woman was, she recognized now, the truth.

———

Normally Helen did not look forward to outings with the martini club—the small talk, the inevitable hangover the following day. But it had been nearly two months since she and Claude had spent an evening together. She hardly saw him on the weekends now that he was involved with a building consortium six hours north, in Jacksonville. Instead, Glenda would phone on Friday afternoons to give Helen his contact information for the weekend.

A week earlier, she had bundled up her shift dresses, trousers with elastic waistbands, and tunic tops and dropped them at Goodwill. Then she had gone shopping at Dillard's, where she bought a sparkling, slinky knit dress that showed off her newly restored curves and firmness. She wanted Claude to notice her.

One of the things she had always loved about Claude, paradoxically, was that he left her alone. In an anthropology text, she had once read about types of marriages and decided theirs was closest to the "boardinghouse." In this paradigm, the couple lived together, loved each other, but remained emotionally separate. Claude had always respected her independence and accepted that she had her own existence—teaching and a rich mental life—apart from him. And, happily, he was not the sort of man who recounted his day at the dinner table. Other than tossing a compliment her way now and then, and throwing a fit over her period, he had barely acknowledged her changes. The new dress would point him toward her main concern: she was indisputably becoming younger by the day.

She and Claude congregated with the other martini club

members in the back room of Fenway's Restaurant to watch the sunset over Lake Withla. Helen felt good in her sexy dress. Claude had told her she looked "gorgeous" when he opened her car door.

The wife of Claude's partner could not get over Helen's appearance. "What have you been doing?" she asked right off the bat.

"Well, you may have heard I retired from teaching. I'm in graduate school now."

"No, I mean what have you been doing to your body?"

"Nothing special," Helen said. The woman looked unsatisfied, so Helen improvised. "Actually, I've been dieting. I've lost a ton of weight." Helen's eyes circled the room. The aging women of southwest Florida were all blonde, the aging men surgically or chemically hirsute. She imagined them converging on her in a peroxided, hair-plugged mob, demanding she divulge her secret. She'd have to lie. She'd already begun to concoct a story about putative stem cell treatments administered in Austria. Or maybe India would be more convincing and harder to verify.

"I see," the woman said, still appraising Helen's looks. "I don't think I'd have recognized you if I hadn't seen you walk in with Claude."

"I love your purse." Helen touched the intricate beading. She could sense the woman's uncontrollable curiosity, her eyes like a beam measuring her brow and neck. "Is it handmade?" Where was Claude? He never used to drift off at parties. Why wasn't he by her side to help fend off her admirers?

"Yes, in Italy." The woman turned the pouch over.

"Beautiful. Excuse me for a moment." Helen gestured toward the ladies' room. "Have to powder my nose. So nice to see you."

After a quick trip to the restroom, she located Claude, chatting in a knot of men. "I need to talk to you," she whispered, standing at his elbow.

"Can it wait until we get home?"

"I'd rather we went outside, if it isn't too buggy."

Claude excused himself and they strolled onto the patio lit with tiki torches and bucket-sized citronella candles. A mosquito zapper glowed bluely at the edge of the lawn.

"It's becoming difficult for me, you know," Helen said.

"What is?"

"Oh, come on, don't act as if you don't know."

Claude insisted on his own stupidity. "Know what?"

"People are starting to wonder why I look so good. And they aren't believing what I tell them. I get the feeling they're angry about it."

"Just tell them you've been to a fat farm or a spa."

"Claude," Helen said, touching his face with both her hands. "Look at me."

He gazed at her, first her face, then her body.

"Keep looking." She slowly pirouetted. "And if you can, tell me what you see."

Claude took his time. He walked around and beheld her from every vantage point.

"Well?"

"I see a stranger." He began to weep.

Two weeks later Helen returned from grocery shopping to find an envelope addressed to her under the amethyst geode on the spinet. The handwriting was Claude's. She tossed her purse and keys onto the end table and sank onto the couch with the letter.

Dear Helen,
     Please forgive me for writing instead of speaking with you.

Out of the corner of her eye, Helen glimpsed Benita washing a window in the sunroom with circular strokes.

I don't know who you are anymore. The younger you look, the older I feel. I am not blind. I see how men are looking at you. Every day, I expect you to dump me for a better offer.

Poor Claude, Helen thought. Poor sweet Claude! She must reassure him immediately. She would never leave Claude, not in a thousand years. The thought shocked her: it would be equivalent to abandoning a child or an aged parent.

I have decided to take matters into my own hands and leave. I've talked with Greg—he understands. I know you'll need some time with this. I hope we can still be friends.
                                                                    Claude

A sob like a leonine roar burst forth from Helen's chest. How could he? He might as well have put a bullet in her head. She felt herself descend into a pit seething with all the loneliness in the world.

Benita approached with a glass of lemon tea for her. "I am so sorry, missus," she said. "I see him packing his clothes." Benita handed Helen a tissue. "The lady was here helping him."

Helen froze, midsob. "What lady?" The first tentacles of rage began to unwind inside her.

"Oh, señora, I am so sorry. I shouldn't have tell you. She kiss him in the kitchen. And the bathroom."

It was probably that new attorney he'd hired. How had he described her? The words leapt to mind as if memorized: *bilingual and quite beautiful.* Helen grabbed Benita's arm. "What did she look like?"

Benita sighed. "Old."

Later, Benita remembered the woman's name: Glenda. Claude's secretary. They used to joke that Glenda was his day wife. Helen had been dumped for an older woman.

———

She cried for days. She wept as if she were sixteen and lovelorn for the first time and also with the rock-solid conviction that this would be the last time anyone broke her heart. At the end of a week of lamentation, she decided to visit Gregory and his family in Seattle. In the mirror, her face continued to youthen, though it was pinched and wan.

She bought an airline ticket for Monday morning. On Sunday afternoon, she phoned to prepare her family for what they would find at the airport. Susan and Gregory, each on an extension, listened in silence as she detailed the extent of her transformation. She reminded them of her youthful appearance at Halloween, summarized her progression in the five months since. "You probably won't recognize me," she warned. "Inside I'm exactly the same. I mean, I haven't forgotten anything, my thoughts are the thoughts of a sixty-four-year-old woman." She paused before dropping the bomb. "But outside, I'm younger than either of you. I think I'm about twenty-six."

"Oh my God," Gregory whispered. "Incredible." At least he took her word for it. Of course he would: he had talked to Claude.

In the background, Helen could hear Evan arguing with his mother. "I want to talk to Big Helen like everybody else," he demanded. She pictured his pert face bunching up, beginning to redden. "Everybody has a phone but me," he screamed at full bore. "Even dumb Little Helen gets to listen."

His mother said, "I just happen to be holding Little Helen, but she is not listening."

"I talk to Grandma. Not you, stupid-head Evan," Little Helen taunted. At which point Evan pitched a full-scale tantrum that momentarily overshadowed the prospect of a twenty-six-year-old grandmother.

"You're my mother," Gregory said finally. "I'm sure we'll spot you. Besides, I've seen plenty of old snapshots of you."

"Listen, I think you should prepare the children if you can. And now, would you please put Evan on the phone?"

She wanted to comfort her grandson, to prepare him for the fact that she would appear to be a total stranger.

Evan waited for everyone to hang up. "I'm coming to the airport in my costume," he told Helen. "Just like you did." His voice squeaked with excitement.

"That's great, Evan. I can't wait to see you. I'm kind of in a costume, too."

"The hula girl?"

"No. A different one." She explained that the costume made her look like someone else, but that he would recognize her by her voice and by all the things she knew about him. She suggested they have a code word, like spies, so that he would know for sure that she was his Big Helen.

"Can I pick the word?" Evan asked.

"Of course you can."

"Goodie," Evan said. "How about 'waffles'? Mom just made some. I have to hang up now, Grandma, my food's getting cold."

"Excellent." Helen jotted the word on a scrap of paper and tucked it into her purse.

━━

That night, while preparing for bed, Helen surveyed herself in the bathroom mirror and noticed a bright spot on one incisor, like the fake twinkles in toothpaste and jewelry commercials. She smiled broadly, her teeth a cavalcade of white, her gums pink and cushiony.

She wrote a note and a check to Benita for a month's worth of housecleaning:

Hola, Benita,

Please do the usual routine, nothing special. I don't know how long I'll be away. Call me at Greg's in Seattle if I'm not back when this check runs out.

Muchas gracias, Helen

She climbed into bed and read until midnight, then slept without interruption or memorable dreams.

She awoke rested and energetic to the six o'clock traffic report. She looked forward to Seattle, with its mossy woodlands and stands of Douglas fir bathed in refreshing mist. Especially to the heavy ground fog that made it possible to move from shadow to shadow without being seen.

Teeth glinting, a primal gleam in her eye, she rummaged through her closet, finding nothing appropriate, nothing that would not crowd the bushy tail that had sprouted overnight at the base of her spine.

A storm of thoughts swirled in her head, emotions heaving and crackling like lightning. *Good-bye, my darlings!* a voice wailed inside the maelstrom.

Wolf pups grew quickly; the dam gave her all and was pregnant again in a year or two. No wrenching departures, none of the prickly love that human mothers endured. *Good-bye, Gregory, Little Helen!*

Her chest felt hollow, as if she were winded.

No more pleasure and pride at graduations and weddings.

No children issuing from children like Russian nesting dolls. All gone. The blood tie, a matter of smell, dissolved when the young became adults and vanished into the scent of strangers. Otherwise, the loss would have been unbearable.

Farewell, Evan! Evan? Even, ever, good-bye, good grrrr. . . .

She stroked the brushy appendage now absently, now proudly, tantalized by its muscularity and sleekness, the glistening fur. As she pushed past trousers and skirts, the tail responded, coiling and uncoiling, lashing from side to side as if it had a mind and heart of its own.

Acknowledgments

I am grateful to the National Endowment for the Arts and to the Florida Arts Council for grants that supported this work, as well as to the Virginia Center for the Creative Arts. Special thanks are due to the editors of the following magazines who first gave these stories a home in their pages: *Epoch; Modern Maturity; Paterson Literary Review; Prairie Schooner; Shenandoah; Tikkun;* and *The Virginia Quarterly Review.*

"The Hottest Spot on Earth" was awarded the 2005 Glenna Luschei Award by *Prairie Schooner.*

"Chosen" was awarded the 2004 Emily Clark Balch Prize for Fiction by *The Virginia Quarterly Review.*

"The Other Mother" was selected for inclusion in *New Stories from the South: 1998, The Year's Best* (Chapel Hill, N.C.: Algonquin Books, 1998).

"Fill In the Blank" was selected for inclusion in *New Stories from the South: 2006, The Year's Best* (Chapel Hill, N.C.: Algonquin Books, 2006).

"The Other Mother" also appeared in *The Orlando Group*

and Friends: A Collection of Writing (Tampa, Fla.: Arbiter Press, 2000).

—

Anika Streitfeld, my editor at Random House, provided indispensable advice in the final shaping of these stories. Thank you, Anika.

Tourist Season

ENID SHOMER

A READER'S GUIDE

A Conversation with Enid Shomer

Maxine Kumin is a Pulitzer Prize–winning poet who has also published five novels and a collection of short fiction. Her sixteenth book of poems is Still to Mow. *She met Enid Shomer in 1984 at the Atlantic Center for the Arts, where Kumin was the Master Artist in Residence and Shomer was one of her fellows. A few years later they began exchanging poems and stories in process. In 1993, Kumin asked Shomer to interview her for* The Massachusetts Review. *They have been friends ever since.*

Q: *Many of these stories are set in Florida. Is this because you consider yourself a native daughter?*

A: Though I wasn't born in Florida, I have spent most of my life here. My grandparents settled in Lemon City in the twenties, and my family visited them for three weeks every summer. From the age of three to four I lived in Florida and it was paradise for a young child—being able to stay outdoors year-round, the swimming, seashells, beaches, fishing, and so on. Still, when I returned as a newlywed, I was amazed to discover that I had a deep visceral attachment to the place. I'd be walking in the evening, for example, and I'd smell night-blooming jasmine and be flooded with memories. It was quite magical. I had come home, to a home I hadn't remembered until I got there.

Q: *Where did you get the idea for the first story in the book, "Chosen"? In that story and in the last story, "Laws of Nature," you leap out of reality and invite us into another reality. How do you feel about these side excursions into other realms?*

A: I got the idea for "Chosen" after listening to an NPR interview with a Tibetan man who was a reincarnated saint. For me, this story doesn't trespass into another realm. I admit it's far-fetched, but it doesn't violate the laws of physics, so it could conceivably happen. But "Laws of Nature" definitely enters another realm, and I was surprised by the direction it took. Both tales began with the same magic word: if. What if a woman began to grow younger instead of older? What if the Tibetan Buddhist powers-that-be concluded that a saint had reincarnated himself as an American speech therapist? I've always been interested in culture-dependent ideas and traditions, even the most profound and absolute ones. For example, for most people religion is determined by the accident of their birth, rather than by choice. But if you believe that religious dogma is universally true across all cultures and is not the expression of a particular history, then couldn't Iris be a Buddhist saint even though she lives in Florida and is Jewish? As for Helen's transformation, I asked myself a similar question: if women in Mexico could turn into pigs and wolves, why couldn't an American woman? Such magic would not be an alternate reality for a reader raised where this folk belief is credible.

That said, I don't want to give the impression that I sat around contemplating these ideas, because I don't intellectualize about or analyze my stories. That just doesn't work for me. I write my way through them, with a little reasoning here and there and in the revision process.

Q: *"You will be a bridge between two cultures," Iris is told in "Chosen," as she and her husband fly back to Florida. There, she resumes her speech therapy classes and introduces Lu and Wangrit to baseball and other things American, but is she acting as that bridge? Did you intend to leave the end of the story somewhat open for your readers?*

A: For me, she *is* acting as that bridge, but being bound in Iris's culture, we don't fully comprehend how that is happening, what her example and her words mean to Lu and Wangrit, the Tibetan messengers. We get the first hint of Iris acting as that bridge earlier in the story, when she addresses the multitudes in Dharamsala. You may recall that she wonders why Lu's translation of her one-sentence remark is so lengthy. Is he embroidering on it? Creating a context for it? More pointedly, at the end of the story, when Lu and Wangrit are living with Iris, and Lu debriefs her at the end of each day, he is finding plenty to record in his lotus-paper notebook.

From the beginning, Lu and Wangrit have been assuring Iris that she doesn't have to think she is wise to be wise. You could explain this apparent contradiction in a couple of ways. First, it is possible to extract deep meaning from simple acts and words. Second, Lu and Wangrit are listening to and observing Iris with different ears and eyes. It's a bit like reading poetry in translation. What we glean from a T'ang dynasty poem by Li Po or from a Rilke sonnet may not be what the poet's contemporaries grasped or even what the poet intended, but in my estimation that doesn't matter much. Like readers, Lu and Wangrit are looking for meaning, for significance, for signposts that point the way. So Iris's words and deeds are weighted heavily in favor of significance from the get-go, and things that she takes for granted and wouldn't consider especially wise may carry profound meaning for the Tibetans.

Q: *My favorite story in the book is "Rapture." The writing is gorgeous, and though there is a very strong narrative thread, it has virtually no plot. Almost nothing happens! Yet I was very sad when I got to the end and realized there was no hope of rescuing Janet, the main character. How did you come to develop this unusual narrative technique?*

A: I wanted to write a story that conveyed a character's life in a short format with very little connective tissue between lyrical passages. We've all heard that when you are dying your whole life flashes before your eyes, but obviously there wouldn't be time for your *whole* life, so instead, maybe just a few disconnected patches would zoom by. I thought the strictures of this form would help to nip in the bud any tendency to be maudlin, which I was concerned about because I'd never killed off a character before. Janet's death is a result of nitrogen narcosis. To complicate things, a prescription drug she has taken amplifies the euphoria that is the first and most insidious symptom of nitrogen narcosis, or "rapture of the deep." She becomes intoxicated at a shallower depth than she would have without this drug concentrated in her blood. When I explain it afterward like this, it sounds so premeditated. Initially, I didn't even connect the title "Rapture" to rapture of the deep, which is not unusual for me since I am always writing out of what I don't know, what mystifies me. In this case, I knew the technique and outcome of the story beforehand, but not the details of Janet's life.

Q: *It's obvious that you're comfortable writing about women and their dilemmas. We see one woman, Sheila, right after her divorce in "The Other Mother," and another, Janet, who is on the verge of divorce in "Rapture." I have to say that I see Sheila as rather helpless. And in fact, I wonder about "Rapture"— why does Janet let herself be taken by the Cayman Trench?*

A: Sheila is resourceful, even spunky, and is fashioning a new identity for herself as so many people have done after a divorce or death or other big shift in their lives. There is nothing in the story to suggest that she will fail. As for Janet in "Rapture," I don't think she "lets herself be taken by the Cayman Trench." But then why, you ask, did she forget to list the drug she takes for her panic disorder? My guess is that she simply forgot. But if you subscribe to the idea that there are no accidents, then you could probably make the case that there is something else afoot in the story. That's one of the wonderful things about fiction for me as a reader and a writer: once these characters come to life, they have the complexity of real human beings and resist being completely transparent. So, there is room for discussion about this, and you could make the case that there is a degree of volition involved in Janet's death. But I don't want to make that case.

Q: *A lot of the men in these stories are cads. Can you explain the difference in your approach to male characters versus the intense and loving scrutiny you give to the women, even to the charming miscreant Garland, who appears in two stories?*

A: With the exception of Clarence in "Sweethearts" and David in "The Summer of Questions," I think the men in the stories are pretty regular fellows. I bring the same scrutiny to all of my characters, but these stories happen to be about the women, who are just as imperfect as the men. None of them are idealized. I suppose this perception depends on how you see their shortcomings. For example, in my view, just because a couple gets divorced after thirty years doesn't mean their whole marriage was a wreck. So Claude in "Laws of Nature," for example, is no villain. He just can't deal with Helen's transformation and he is scared. He does the thing that he is afraid will be done to him.

Q: *In "Sweethearts" and in "Fill in the Blank," Garland breaks the law. She commits robbery, and of course she*

shoplifts. Earlier, she committed arson. In "The Other Mother"
you have another instance of law-breaking, and this time it's
far more serious than any of Garland's misdeeds. Do these
crimes hold a special fascination for you?

A: No, but I did begin to wonder if a person could slide into
crime sideways, which is how I suspect it must happen for
some people. With Garland, I wanted to explore how a gutsy
young woman who intends no harm could fall into the habit
of wrongdoing for reasons that have nothing to do with being
attracted to crime. I knew she was scarred by the death of her
mother. For example, without being aware of it, she believes
that, like her mother, she, too, will die young. Often people hold
beliefs or make assumptions they are unaware of. I mean, isn't
that the big insight of more than a century of psychology—
that human beings are not cognizant or in control of their
emotions and often act without understanding their motives?
This is nothing new, but it is profound. The recognition that
the unconscious mind is a vast labyrinth that is difficult to access is Freud's biggest contribution to our understanding of
human nature. One reason I love the Greek tragedies is that
they show us in a beautiful and thrilling way that even when
people are warned of what they will do, as Oedipus is, it
doesn't help. Because we can't untangle our own motives, we
are constantly surprised by our emotional responses to events.
We may be convinced that we understand other people's motives and behavior, but frequently our theories turn out to be
edifices of self-serving baloney. And our own transgressions
can be just as mysterious.

Q: *We never meet "the other mother" in the story of that name. Did you think about possibly developing her story side by side with Sheila's?*

A: No, I never considered writing from the biological mother's viewpoint. I left her vague intentionally. I wanted her to be a sad and mysterious presence haunting Sheila's world. There's only one description of her, invented by Sheila. She is sitting at a table with her back to Sheila, "her body sagging in a series of interrupted curves." Other than recoiling in pain at the thought of her plight, like Sheila, I don't know any particulars about "the other mother." Maybe she'll appear in a future story.

Q: *We're longtime friends and we're very comfortable sharing poems and stories and neither of us sees a sharp demarcation between genres. In other words, we agree that writing is seamless. Do you think we're in the minority with this notion?*

A: Perhaps. I know of many writers who would disagree. Worse yet, when they hear a statement like you just made, they misinterpret it to mean that we are saying that poetry and fiction are the same. I don't believe that at all! Poetry and fiction are distinctly different. But for me, *writing* fiction or poetry or nonfiction is all part of the same thing—making art. When I teach as a visiting writer or at a conference, I am always surprised at the small number of students who sign up for courses outside their genre. I find it shocking when prose writers tell me they don't read poetry or vice versa, as if two different languages were involved, as if one wrote fiction in English and poetry in Polish. To me, that's like saying that the backstroke and the freestyle aren't both swimming. It's all swimming and it's all writing.

Q: *Have you been able to move out of a story in progress and into a poem and back? For me it's often a relief to move out of one form and into another, and I go back refreshed.*

A: Yes, that has happened frequently. Each gives tang to the other, like a good pickle. Writing poetry also helps to keep my prose concise. Most of all, poetry teaches the power of imagery, which for me is the heart of good writing. Metaphor can grasp and convey subtleties and essences that reason and logic can't touch.

Q: *I like "Sweethearts." The description of Garland going upriver seemed very real to me. It gave me goose bumps to read about her motoring up there all alone at night with her dog. The Southern rivers are scarier than our Yankee rivers. I like the fact, too, that she sees an opening and takes the initiative and drives her enemies off into the night. But her boyfriend is a scumbag. And her father . . . there's another unhappy man who has failed in his life. How do you view male/female relationships?*

A: Though I haven't always been lucky, I suppose I'm still a romantic! I think there are things about her father, Eastman, that Garland doesn't absorb or appreciate. For example, he gives her a gold necklace that belonged to her mother. For a man who is still in mourning, still clinging to the memory of his dead wife, it's enormously important that he gives this relic to his daughter, thereby affirming his love for her. But Garland doesn't get it, isn't moved by it. He isn't a perfect parent, but who is? He's struggling. He's never recovered from the death of his wife and he's cowed by his willful, rebellious daughter.

Q: *Are any of these stories autobiographical in whole or in part? How much do you write out of your own experience?*

A: "Crash Course" is the most autobiographical story in the book. I had an automobile accident like the one in the story. Soon after, I tried to interest the *New York Times* in an essay about the incident, but the editor I queried said, "Oh, another drug dealer who'll be dead by the age of thirty. Nobody wants to read that again." That broke my heart and I determined to write the story as fiction. It's probably a better medium for it anyway.

I don't often write fiction directly from my own experience, but there are cannibalized bits of my life in the stories. For example, I once worked in an all-female bookkeeping department similar to the one in "The Summer of Questions." While living in southwest Florida for nearly two years, I was appalled by the ferocity of land development there and I used that stance for the character Helen in "Laws of Nature." The imagination is powerful, it is godlike, but it can't invent everything from whole cloth, so I also do research to furnish the specific details that create authenticity. It drives me crazy to find a factual error when I'm reading fiction. It ruins the illusion. For "Chosen," I researched Tibet and Tibetan Buddhism. In creating the character Frieda in "Tourist Season," I drew upon knowledge of the Women's Airforce Service Pilots (WASP) that I'd accumulated in writing a poem-biography of the WASP founder, Jacqueline Cochran My stories are always a synthesis of imagination, research, and my own experience.

Q: *I think you depict older women very successfully. Where do these portrayals of older women come from?*

A: I'm not quite sure. I simply became interested in them, and older men, too, maybe because, as Helen says in "Laws of Nature," at a certain point, people become invisible. As more of us live longer, I think we'll be hearing a lot about older women and men. They will move from the edges to the center of stories. Also, I'm past the half-century mark myself, so I'm becoming more personally aware of these issues. Now that we are talking about age, I bet older women are underrepresented in fiction, but I wasn't trying to address that.

Q: *Undoubtedly they are. And that may be what makes older women characters more interesting to read about.*

You also seem very much at home differentiating between the concerns of younger women and older women, and perhaps we notice the differences more because the collection has women of all ages. Garland and Riva are both young, about twenty. Iris and Janet and Sheila are in their forties and fifties, and then there are much older women, like Frieda and Helen, who are in their sixties and seventies. Did you make a decision to include stories about women of all ages, and if so, why?

A: It's interesting that the age of the women keeps coming up when people talk to me about this collection, since not all the women in the book are old, as you rightly point out. Despite the range of ages, I guess the overall impression is not of ingenues. I was pleased when I realized that there were characters from nearly every decade of life. I added a couple of stories to strengthen that balance.

You know, there's a new axiom being touted widely that "sixty is the new forty." That's part of the recognition that with longevity, people can continue to lead interesting lives. The paradigm of a life is no longer birth/adventure-filled youth/marriage/death. There's a huge space opening up between "marriage" and "death" and that's where most of us are now located, and perhaps our literature is beginning to reflect that. I once read the most telling statistic: up until the twentieth century, nine out of ten novels ever written ended with a marriage, everything from the classics by Jane Austen and Charlotte Brontë, to formulaic bodice-rippers. But these days, it's almost as if people get to live more than one lifetime. Many people have two or three careers, multiple marriages, blended families. It will be exciting, I think, to get that retrospective, longer view in fiction. It will be a new category of wisdom, a new flavor of it, if you will.

Q: *I love the ambition and reach of "The Hottest Spot on Earth"; you combine pornography with civil disobedience, rivalry between your women protagonists with social commentary on the mass destruction brought about by nuclear explosions. The depiction of the nuclear resisters being arrested over and over makes a statement that readers can interpret on their own. Is this a futile gesture or a necessary brave one? And then we are in Patricia's head as she ponders what insight she can take from this day. She considers the possibility of an article titled "Who Protests for Pornography?" For me, this epitomized the shallowness of trying to invent a scholarly thesis from the whole porn industry, and I laughed out loud. How seriously did you take the Slash writers' convention, and where did you get the germ for it?*

A: "The Hottest Spot on Earth" grew out of a lecture I attended on Slash pornography. Before then, I didn't know that Slash existed. Around the same time, I taught a poetry workshop in Las Vegas and was struck by the great smorgasbord of people I encountered there. I thought Las Vegas would be the perfect setting for a Slash convention. Contrast and contradiction were the delights for me in writing this story—between the two women, between the protesters and the pornographers, the feminism of Dr. Warde and her seductive, ultra-feminine wardrobe, and so on. I enjoy cultural collisions and disconnects. A while back I read somewhere that a pasture was mistakenly rented out for a Renaissance fair and a Civil War battle reenactment on the same weekend. I loved the thought of that, of women wearing wimples bumping up against soldiers in blue and gray. I love the idea of people pursuing their idiosyncratic passions and I take them very seriously. This includes Trekkies at Star Trek conventions, toy train collectors, orchid fanciers and dog agility teams, scholarly societies, and clubs that study Depression glass. All these allegiances are enriching. Maybe they contribute to American society being well-ventilated and susceptible to new ideas.

Q: *I laughed out loud many times in reading your book. How do you account for the humor?*

A: Sometimes the humor really takes me by surprise, because I approach every story with such seriousness of purpose. I remember the first time I read a story aloud. At one point I had to pause to wait for the audience to finish laughing. "What?" I thought to myself. "This funeral scene is funny?" I almost never sit down thinking, Now I am going to write a funny story. Humor finds its way organically into some stories and that, I think, is when it's best.

Q: *What are you working on now?*

A: I'm writing a historical novel, set in Egypt in 1849. Florence Nightingale and Gustave Flaubert are the protagonists. Though they never met that we know of in real life, they both set sail down the Nile on the same day and followed identical itineraries. Imagine the possibilities!

Reading Group Questions
and Topics for Discussion

1. A strong sense of place has traditionally been important in Southern fiction. What role does the state of Florida play in this collection? Can you imagine these stories taking place in another part of the country?

2. What makes these stories especially modern in your view? Why couldn't *Tourist Season* have been written fifty years ago?

3. Shomer's stories have been described as both poignant and humorous. How would you characterize the humor and how is it connected to the serious drama?

4. In "Chosen," Iris Hornstein travels to Tibet to don the mantle of a reincarnated Buddhist saint. Can you imagine this happening to anyone you know? What does this story suggest about religion?

5. In "The Other Mother," Sheila learns the true story behind Royal's adoption when Royal is nearly an adult. How do you

think Sheila would have reacted if she had learned the truth when Royal was much younger?

6. What impels Garland McKenney, the protagonist of both "Fill In the Blank" and "Sweethearts," to commit her crimes? What do you think might prevent her in the future?

7. In the story "Tourist Season," what do you think Frieda means when she tells Milt, "We're both like Knoblock"? How would you characterize Frieda and Milt's marriage? How does Frieda's work as a Women's Airforce Service Pilot affect her life and their relationship?

8. In "Rapture" we learn that Janet "hardly ever referred to herself as an artist or to her work as art," yet her show tours the South and is featured in an important art magazine. How do you explain this discrepancy? Do you think it is related to her fate?

9. "The Hottest Spot on Earth" alternates between two points of view, which is rare in a short story. Why do you think the author chose this technique rather than tell the story from a single viewpoint? What pulls Jill and Patricia together and what pushes them apart?

10. A key aspect of "Sweethearts" is Garland's relationship to Carlene, the housekeeper. What role does race play in this story?

11. How would you describe Abby Presner's behavior toward the unnamed young man in "Crash Course"? Why do you think she doesn't get frightened until after the incident?

12. In "The Summer of Questions," Riva unravels secrets she hadn't even suspected existed. What mysteries does she solve and which remain? At the end of the story Alma says, "When you're not being beautiful, make trouble." What would Riva's likely response to this be?

13. Do you believe that Helen in "Laws of Nature" is actually becoming younger, or did you read this story as a metaphor or fable? What do you think the author intended? Which other stories address the aging process?

14. What role do marriage and work play in these stories? In which stories are the two at war with each other, and in which do they coexist more happily? If you are married, what is the relationship between marriage and work in your own life?

15. The women in *Tourist Season* range from seventeen to over seventy. What differences do you see between the younger and the older protagonists? What do they have in common? Why do you think the author chose to include women of such a wide age range in the same collection?

16. If you could be any of the women in these stories, which would you choose? Which character did you most closely identify with?

17. Iris in "Chosen," Sheila in "The Other Mother," Garland in "Sweethearts," and Helen in "Laws of Nature" all leave their old lives behind and find new ones. Do the catalysts for change come from within the women, or does environment or circumstance effect the need for change? What do you think might cause you to change your own life so drastically?

18. In what ways are the characters in these stories all tourists in their own lives?

PHOTO: BETH KELLY

ENID SHOMER'S stories and poems have appeared in *The New Yorker*, *The Paris Review*, and *The Atlantic Monthly*, among other publications. She is the recipient of grants from the National Endowment for the Arts and the Florida Arts Council, and her debut collection, *Imaginary Men*, won the Iowa Short Fiction Award and the LSU/*Southern Review* Award. Two of these stories have been selected for *New Stories from the South: The Year's Best*. Shomer lives in Tampa, Florida, and is currently at work on a novel.